RED HOTT AND WILDER

A STEAMY HOLIDAY COLLECTION

SERENA BELL

JMG
JELSBA
MEDIA
GROUP

PART I

HOT UNDER THE COLLAR

1

REGGIE

This is so not me.

Before today, I would have told you that "self-care" was a concept for people who had too much time on their hands. I would have said candles were for religious services, and the removable nozzle on the shower was to clean the grout in hard-to-reach locations.

But my therapist told me this morning I have to do a better job of treating myself the way I deserve to be treated, so here I am. Trying, at least.

Because I *do* deserve way better than the bullshit deal I've gotten this year: My ex-husband leaving me for a twenty-four-year-old dance teacher, the two of them moving together to Santorini to lie on Mediterranean beaches and bonk each other's brains out.

I definitely deserve better than that.

I'm willing to try this "treating myself well" for one night, if only as a fuck-you to them.

On my way back to work from my therapy visit, I bought tea lights at the grocery store, and when I got home,

I dug out all the candles I own. There were two scented candles I got as gifts from people who clearly don't know me very well, and a novelty candle shaped like a well-endowed penis—a gift from someone who clearly *does* know me.

I arrange candles in my bedroom, trailing them into the bathroom, around the sink and tub. The dick candle goes in a place of honor on my nightstand. I mean, right?

I have to admit, the whole effect is pretty. And peaceful.

I climb into the tub. The water is blissfully warm.

Okay, this self care thing doesn't totally suck.

The water slooshes over me, covering my belly and setting my breasts afloat. It feels really good. At my therapist's suggestion, I've kept the shower nozzle within arm's length, and I reach for it now and turn on the water. Mmm... that's...

Whoa.

That's really good.

Way better than anything my ex ever came up with.

I am officially a self-care convert!

In the other room, I hear the Roomba leave its dock and start pacing my bedroom, but I ignore it, because the ticklish, delicious sensation of the water between my legs is waaaay too distracting.

I'm going to give my therapist a raise.

I brace my feet on the tub floor and lift my hips to make the spray of the nozzle more direct. And ohhhhhhhh.

A piercing sound stabs my ears and floods the room. What the—

I sit bolt upright, dropping the sprayer into the tub. And then I smell it.

Smoke.

I haul myself out of the tub and race into the bedroom. Holy shit; the Roomba has knocked over one of my tea lights and set the carpet and the bottom of my bedskirt on fire. I run back into the bathroom, looking around frantically for something I can fill with water. I dump tea lights in the sink and fill two small glasses with water, but by the time I get back to the bedroom, the water merely sizzles and steams on the fire.

Stay calm! Think!

It's harder than it sounds when your bed is on fire. And not in the good way.

I need a big bucket. Or...

Fire extinguisher!

I run downstairs to the kitchen, grab the fire extinguisher, and race back up. I yank the pin, squeeze the handle and—

Whoosh.

A moment later, the world settles.

The fire's out. The room is full of smoke, yellow powder everywhere, the smell of ammonia slicing through my brain. I grab the Roomba—which has miraculously evaded the fire—and power it off, then back away from the disaster, hovering outside the door of the bedroom.

As I stand there, panting, my heart gradually slows to a trot. And then—as my brain begins to process again—I hear it.

The fire alarm is still screeching.

Shit.

And then, below the shrill cry...

Sirens.

Noooo.

I totally forgot: The fire alarms in my house are wired into the central security system, which means when the alarm sounds for more than ninety seconds, it calls the fire department.

Red light floods the bedroom, turning the yellow-powdered floor orange.

Fists pound my front door.

I duck into the bedroom and grab the first clothes I can find—sleep shorts that haven't fit me since Obama was president and the nearest t-shirt, which happens to say *The boobs are real, the smile is fake*—yanking them onto my still slightly damp body.

I race down the stairs and come face to face with two firefighters in full gear, masks down. Shit shit shit.

"The fire's out!" I tell them.

"Where was it?" one asks.

"Uh," I say, because all of a sudden I remember:

Tub full of water.

Shower nozzle dropped in the tub.

Water still on.

Candles still burning (didn't have time to blow them out —too busy worrying about not setting entire house on fire, and shutting down Roomba so it wouldn't set anything else on fire).

"Where was the fire?" the same one demands, which is when I notice that even in a helmet he's distressingly good looking. At least six-three, with broad shoulders the gear can't hide, full lips, warm brown eyes, and a chiseled jaw.

And he's about to climb the stairs and see my nest o' self lovin'.

"Ma'am," he says, which kinda, I won't lie, makes me want to die, even though in fairness he's definitely younger than I am. "Please."

I point up the stairs.

He indicates my front door. "Out," he says. "Go stand in the street till we give you the all clear."

I definitely shouldn't think his commanding attitude is hot. Not after almost immolating myself in an autoerotic fire.

It probably doesn't help that I was seven-eighths of the way to orgasm and am pumped full of adrenaline.

I obey the sexy command and head outside. It's September, the evenings starting to cool off, and my nipples tighten. I look down. The water dripping off my hair has left wet patches on my well-worn, light-colored t-shirt.

I am...

Highly visible.

I should have gone ahead and died when the sexy firefighter called me "ma'am," because I'm going to die of embarrassment anyway.

I bury my face in my hands.

My neighbors gather, drawn by the sirens and lights, concerned; I cross my arms so I don't give *them* a show, too. My eighty-year-old next door neighbor drapes a hot pink fuzzy sweater around my shoulders, and I thank her, pulling it tight around my *The boobs are real* headlights. She and my other neighbors clamor for info, and I lie and say I burned a pizza (seriously, can you blame me?). Thankfully, they lose interest and drift away.

The firefighters finish their work and come outside; it's just me now, and the not-as-sexy firefighter (he's still good eye candy) gives me a tight nod and heads back to the truck.

The hot firefighter has taken his helmet off. His hair is dark and neatly trimmed, high and tight, the edges all precise and baring a thin line of skin that's whiter than his seasonal tan. I recognize the haircut and him at the same moment: He's one of Mei's clients at the day spa and salon where I work. Greeaaatt, so on top of everything, I'll actually have to see him again.

Unless I hide the next time he comes in, which seems like an excellent idea.

"The fire's definitely out," he says. "It didn't reach the mattress, which is extremely good news because if it had, we'd have had to douse the mattress to make sure it was really out. Good work with the extinguisher."

I wasn't expecting praise, and for some reason— possibly my ludicrous outfit and tight nipples, possibly because he knows I was worshipping at the altar of the dick candle *with my shower nozzle attachment*—I blush.

He crosses his arms, and the stern expression on his face gives me fantasy material for the next time I'm foolish enough to take my therapist's advice. "I turned off the water and put the rest of your candles out. I'm going to give you the standard candle safety lecture. Always keep a burning candle within sight." He ticks it off on his fingers, which are long, blunt-tipped, and visibly calloused. My still alert girl-parts give a needy squeeze. "Extinguish all candles when leaving a room or before going to sleep." He gives me a look that I'm pretty sure says that this also encompasses wanking in the bathtub. "Never burn a candle on or near anything that can catch fire."

Never burn a candle shaped like a big penis, just in case you set your house on fire and a hot firefighter comes to put it out.

"I don't usually—candles aren't—that's not—" I give up. "I, uh—I'm so sorry."

Death, I am yours.

He waves a hand. "All part of the job. A few tips on fire extinguisher cleanup. We'll take the spent one with us, but you obviously need to get a replacement ASAP. Vacuum up the contents—wear a mask when you do that, and make sure you use a vacuum with a filter. You can use isopropyl alcohol diluted 50 percent with warm water to get the stuck-on residue."

"Thank you," I manage.

His eyes meet mine, and the corner of his mouth turns up. "I'd say the pleasure was all mine," he says, "but I'm guessing maybe it wasn't."

Then he turns and walks back to the truck, leaving me with my mouth hanging open.

2

FORD

Since the fire at her place, I've been to Hott Spot three times for a trim.

Reggie never cuts my hair.

Even when Reggie's the one who greets me at the front desk, she always finds a way to turn me over to the other stylist, Mei. Who is very pretty and gives great haircuts.

But she's not Reggie—whose name I only know because I asked Mei.

Today I'm determined: This is the day Reggie will cut my hair, I'll chat her up, and I'll ask her out.

When I push through the front door of the day spa and salon, the first thing I see is a flash of Reggie's multicolored hair behind the main desk. As I get closer, she sits up, giving me a better view of her heart-shaped face—round cheeks, slightly pointed chin, pierced eyebrows, and sparkling nose ring.

I know from talking to her the night of her candle fire that there's also a stud in her tongue.

I've thought about that tongue stud a lot.

"Hey!" I say.

She looks up. "Hi, can I help you?"

She either doesn't recognize me or is pretending not to know me. Fair enough. I might too if I were in her shoes. I know she was embarrassed the night we answered the call at her house and caught her in the middle of—

Well, the middle of whatever she'd been in the middle of.

I've thought about that a lot, too. A lot. Couldn't stop thinking about how she never got to finish, and I've pictured a thousand ways I could help her with that. My dreams have been full of ideas.

"I'm here for a haircut," I say. "I don't know if you remember me—"

"Mei usually cuts your hair, right?" she says, keying through something on the computer, staring at it like it's the most fascinating thing she's ever seen.

"You cut, too, right? That would work, if you're available."

"Let me just see if Mei's available," she says, like she didn't even hear me.

"Hey—not sure if you remember, but I answered the call at your house the night of the fire," I say.

"I know," she says. Grudgingly, like she was *really* hoping I wouldn't go there. She looks back at the computer screen. "Ah. You're in luck. Mei will be free after this slot, in about five minutes. I'm booking you in with her—"

"About that night—"

Her eyes flash. "Can we *please* not talk about it? Don't you have some kind of confidentiality agreement? Aren't you under some oath not to discuss the weird-ass shit you see when you show up at someone's house in the middle of the night and catch them worshipping at the altar of dick?"

I laugh. I can't help it.

She scowls at me. "If our situations were reversed, you wouldn't want to talk about it either."

"I don't own a dick candle."

She snorts, and her gaze flicks to mine briefly, appreciatively.

"Hope this isn't too weird a question—"

"Anything that starts that way is definitely too weird," she says.

I laugh, then open my mouth to continue. But at that moment, Mei steps into the reception area with a client at her side. Nan.

"Ford Cartright! What brings you here?" Nan demands.

Nan's the grandmother of one of my crewmates, and I spent so much time in her house growing up that she might as well have been my grandmother. She's a seventy-ish plump woman with a head of soft, fluffy white hair. She also owns one of Rush Creek's two bakeries, and she created Rush Creek's now infamous Better-Than-Sex cake, which she calls Better-Than-Robert-Redford cake (even though everyone in town knows it by its real name).

"Hey, Nan. This," I say, gesturing to my hair, which is more loose and scruffy than high and tight.

She scrutinizes me. "Yeah, that could use some TLC."

Nan always tells it like it is.

"You waiting for Mei?" she asks me.

"Uh—"

No-win situation here: I can't say in front of Mei that I

don't want her to cut my hair, but if I keep my mouth shut, Reggie will definitely pawn me off on Mei.

Nan looks from Reggie to me and back again, the corners of her mouth tilting up. Uh-oh. Nan is a notorious busybody, and that smile scares me.

"You going to the Hott & Cold Holiday Festival?" she asks Reggie.

I give Nan a quelling look, which has zero effect. Subtlety doesn't work with Nan.

"Wasn't planning on it," Reggie says, shrugging.

"I'm going." Mei smiles at Nan. "I think it sounds like so much fun!"

"So much," Nan says. She addresses Reggie again. "You love dogs, don't you?"

"You know I do," Reggie says, and her mouth curves in the first smile I've ever seen on her face. And is that a dimple?

It is. I'm such a goner.

"The festival promotes pet adoption and raises money for the Rush Creek Animal Shelter. Look," Nan says, grabbing her phone. "Look at this guy." She taps, scrolls, taps again, then holds the phone out.

Whoa. What's her game? I'm pretty sure I know what's on that screen, even before I crane my neck to confirm my suspicions.

Yup.

I close my eyes and shake my head.

"I know you lost Fargo earlier this year," Nan says sympathetically to Reggie. "So tough, right? Losing Marcus was harder than losing my husband." She pauses. "Much harder, actually." She points to the phone screen. "This guy's named Wags. Not too big, not too small—I met him last week. You'll love him."

"I'm not ready," Reggie says flatly.

"You never *think* you're ready," Nan says. "But have a look at this guy."

I open my eyes to see Nan pushing the phone into Reggie's hands. Reggie looks from Nan's phone screen to me.

"Is that you?" she asks, pointing to the screen.

"Uh, yeah," I say.

The photo is one of twelve in our Adopt-a-Pet, Win-a-Date campaign. Everyone who adopts a pup gets a date to the Hott & Cold Festival—with a firefighter. I wait for Nan to explain the setup.

She doesn't.

Okay, then. *I'll* explain to Reggie that if she adopts Wags, she'll also win a date with me to the Festival. And how much I'd like that.

"So you know the deal with this, right?" I ask Reggie. "The Adopt-a-Pet, Win-a—"

"Is he a good boy?" Reggie interrupts. Her eyes are fixed on the screen, and I'm positive it's not because it's a great photo of me. There's a softness in her eyes as she touches a finger to the photo, right on the little dog's nose. She raises her chin and looks up at the three of us. Her gaze is distant, still soft.

Damn, she's adorable. My train of thought gets hopelessly derailed by the longing on her face.

I'd guess she's been lonely. And that's bullshit, if you ask me. I don't know her well, but that night at her house I learned a few things, and I liked everything I saw.

I want to get to know her better.

She's still waiting for my answer. What was the question? Oh, right:

"Yeah, Wags. *Such* a good boy. The thing is, it's an adoption drive with a twist. If you adopt Wags, you automatically get a daaa—"

"Wags is a *total* sweetheart, isn't he, Ford?" Nan interrupts. "I heard Elsa Craig say she was going to try to adopt him this afternoon. After lunch, I think. So if you're interested, you should go right now, before he gets snatched up—"

Reggie shoves the phone at Nan. "Mei, can you take Ford?" she demands.

Well. Good to know that in a photograph that contains both me and Wags, Wags is the one who prompts immediate action...

"Sure," Mei says, shrugging.

Reggie is already heading toward the back of the spa. "Is Sonya in her office?"

"I think so?" Mei says. "Ford, follow me."

"Reggie, you should know—" I start.

"Oh!" Nan says, bringing her phone up suddenly to her eyes, in a dramatic rendition of someone who's just gotten a text. "Elsa is leaving to go to the shelter right now!"

"Reggie," I attempt again. "It's win a date with a—"

"Gotta run!" she says, and blows past me toward the back of the spa.

I glower at Nan.

"Don't look at me like that," she says. "I just did you a huge favor. You think when she said she wasn't ready, she meant for a dog?" She gives me a hard look. "She meant for *you*. If you'd asked her out, she would have run the other way so fast…"

"So you tricked her. And she's going to feel like *I* tricked her. Not cool."

"'The ends justify the means,'" Nan quotes.

"This is small town dating, Nan, not fifteenth century politics. Pretty sure the tactics are different."

"Machiavelli is always in style."

I shake my head, disgusted.

Mei clears her throat, and I give her a pleading look.

She puts her hands up. "I didn't hear anything," she says, with a sigh. "Ford, come on, let's do something about that hair. You have a festival to go to and my prickly coworker to woo. Can't have you looking like something the dog dragged in."

3

REGGIE

I kneel in the shelter's meet-and-greet room, and Wags climbs onto my lap, puts his paws on my shoulders, and licks my face.

"Hi, Wags, you good boy," I say, and his tail wags furiously.

He has short, light-colored hair and an elegant pointy nose, and he's skinny, whippet-like, but a little more substantial. He turns around once in my lap and settles, and I stroke his head, while his panting slows and his eyes close.

Pretty sure I'm in love.

Sonya, the manager of Hott Spot and one of my closest friends, leans against the wall watching us.

"I don't know," I tell her, even though I do. I totally know. "What if he doesn't get along with Gus?"

Gus is Sonya's dog, and he frequently comes to work with her.

"They don't have to *live* together," she points out. "I'm sure we can figure out how to keep them apart if they don't like each other. But the shelter says Wags gets along with all the other dogs, and Gus gets along with everything and everybody. Groundhogs. Squirrels. My Uncle Ernest. They'll be fine." She watches me a moment more. "You guys look pretty happy together."

The shelter manager, Carol, comes back, takes a look at Wags and me, and grins. "Can I take that as a yes?" she asks.

"You can take it as a hell yes." I scritch Wags's ears, and he sinks a little deeper into me. I don't want to get up and disturb him, but I do want to finish my adoption transaction before Elsa Craig shows up and contests my ownership.

Carol leashes Wags and leads the three of us to the front desk, where I fill out paperwork. She gives me a bunch of handouts with instructions for what to buy and how to help him with the adjustment.

"Oh," she says, consulting something on her computer screen. "He's part of the Adopt-and-Win drive."

"Oh, yeah, Ford said something about that."

"'Ford?'" Sonya echoes. "You mean the hot firefighter? I thought we were here because of something Nan said?"

"Well, Ford just said—"

But I can't remember what Ford said. Just that there had been some urgency in his voice—but it had been drowned out by the urgency in Nan's, and my own need to claim Wags.

As if he can feel it, Wags leans his weight against my leg and gives a little sigh.

"G'boy," I tell him, and he sighs again.

"You two," Sonya says. "You're the cutest thing I've ever seen."

"Oh, right," Carol says, consulting her screen again. "Ford Cartwright was matched up with Wags. Lucky you." She beams at me. "He's definitely the hottest one."

"Hottest—?"

"Hottest firefighter." She rustles in a drawer. "Here you go."

I look down at the item in my hand. It's a bright red ticket to the Hott & Cold Festival. *Ford Cartwright Plus One*, it says.

"What's this?" I ask.

"Your ticket to the festival. As Ford's date."

Sonya makes a choked sound behind me.

"As—what?"

"The Adopt-a-Pup and Win-a-Date adoption drive," Carol says patiently. "Ford's your date."

I shove the ticket across the desk like it burned me. "No," I say. "No, thanks. I'll just take Wags here, and Ford can—Ford can sponsor another pup. No date."

"Wait," Sonya says. "You're turning down a date with the hot firefighter?" She gives me a hard look. She's seen me crushing on him, and has tried to convince me to poach him from Mei—as a client, that is—cut his hair, and ask him out.

She's convinced it's some kind of Samson and Delilah thing. Cut his hair, win his heart. That's what happened with her and her boyfriend Quinn, who she's head over heels about.

But ever since the night of the fire, I've been even more sure that will never happen.

Sonya, as always, looks super hot today. She's wearing a vivid cranberry tank, a pair of fitted pants, and a drapey jacket. A few weeks ago I cut her thick, straight brown hair in a short bob, and it *always* looks good. Whereas my mane of chaos always looks like I slept on it, forgot to brush it, and dipped it in a paint palette.

That last part's on purpose. The rest is just my fate. The rainbow is supposed to distract from the mess—no idea if it works. Basically, I'm jealous of everything about Sonya's appearance today, because she's not-yet-thirty and super hot, and I'm forty and feeling especially blobby since my ex absconded to Santorini.

"There's no way I'm going to that festival with him," I tell her.

"Give us a moment?" she asks Carol.

Carol tries to hide a smile. "Of course."

Sonya grabs my arm and pulls me to the side, Wags trailing obediently at my heel. "Reggie. What the heck? I know you think he's hot."

I sigh. I've never told anyone this story, but I trust Sonya. She won't laugh at me.

Much.

"You have to promise not to tell anyone."

"Cross my heart," she says, doing it.

Wags turns around a few times and settles at my feet, head on my Doc Martens.

"It was a few months ago. I was trying to take my therapist's advice and, you know, practice *self care*."

I hope she won't make me elaborate.

Luckily, Sonya is a woman of great sensitivity, and she gets it. "Faulty toy?" she asks. "I read a great romance novel where the heroine sets a dumpster on fire with her vibrator. Christina Hovland's *It Doesn't Have to Be This Hard.*"

"Um," I say. "No. Not a toy. Well. Not exactly." I close one eye, wincing. "Shower nozzle," I whisper.

"Oh, yeah," she says. "Amen."

"I was in the bathtub. But I lit candles—my therapist's suggestion. In the bathroom and the bedroom. The Roomba... knocked over a candle. The curtains went up in flames. The fire department came. Including. Hot Firefighter."

"Oh," says Sonya. "Oh, *my*."

She's trying really hard not to laugh. I give her an A for effort.

"There was a big dick candle burning on my nightstand. And I may or may not have left the shower nozzle running in the tub when I climbed naked out of it to put out the fire. And then grabbed the closest clothes I could find and put them on while I was still wet. No bra and my *The boobs are real, the smile is fake* t-shirt. It was your basic damp white t-shirt situation."

"Right," Sonya says. "So, that was a little embarrassing."

"A little embarrassing is when you accidentally set your kitchen on fire because you leave the toast in the toaster. This was..." I roll my eyes.

"Was he nice about it?"

"He was professional about it," I say. "Mostly."

She raises her eyebrows.

"As he was walking out, he said, 'I'd say the pleasure was all mine, but I'm guessing maybe it wasn't.'"

"Reggie!" she says. "He likes you!"

"He doesn't," I retort. "I was a hot mess who'd just set her house on fire while making it abundantly clear that her best bet for orgasm this century was herself. Anyway," I say, crossing my arms, "he's too young for me."

Wags whines in agreement.

She squints at me. "You don't know that."

"There's no way he's more than thirty-two, and I'm forty."

"That's not that big an age difference."

"It's an eternity."

She rolls her eyes.

"I'm not his type, anyway."

"How do you *know* that?"

"Come on, Sonya. Him: solid t-shirt, Carhartt jeans, work boots, high-and-tight haircut. Guessing former enlisted? Me: tattoos, ragbag quilt hair, piercings every-where, and—" I look down to see what I'm wearing. Denim mini, ripped tights—it's too cold for fishnets—and this studded leather vest thing I got for, no joke, twelve bucks at Goodwill. I don't bother to finish the sentence. If she can't see that one of these things is not like the other, we're not having this conversation.

Her eyebrows are all scrunched up, WTF-style. She still looks way too unconvinced. "That's a lot of reasons *not to*," she says.

"Exactly."

"But you only need one reason *to*."

"What's that?"

"That you *want* to."

It's my turn to give her the WTF face.

"Just saying, Reggie. Maybe self care in this situation is letting yourself have what you know you want."

I grumble, under my breath, "Or maybe it's *not* doing something you know will end in pain and humiliation."

She presses her lips together like she's trying not to say what she's thinking, then ruins it by saying it anyway.

"I know your ex did a number on you," she says. "But you're beautiful and funny and smart and any man would be lucky to have you."

"I'm forty and desperately in need of a glow-up, and my self-confidence took a sabbatical of unknown duration to Santorini."

She giggles and says, "I rest my case."

"'Funny,' I'll grant you."

"Just give this a chance, hon. Just a chance."

"He saw me basically naked with wet hair wearing a see-through *The boobs are real, the smile is fake* t-shirt, having just made a fool of myself while jerking off in a bathtub with a dick candle on my nightstand," I review for her.

"So he's seen you at your worst and he still liked you enough to flirt with you."

"He wasn't flirting. He was issuing a parting shot. And oh, my God, Sonya, if I accept this date, he's going to think I raced out of the salon to get a date with him!"

"So tell him the truth. That you fell in love with the dog and had no idea it was a package deal."

I groan. Wags lifts his head, making sure everything's okay. "I'm good, bud," I tell him, and he lowers it again.

"Ugh," I say. "This is lose-lose, isn't it? If I keep Wags—"

Wags lifts his head again, giving me worried eyes.

" which obviously I am," I quickly amend. "Sorry, dude. That was thoughtless of me. *Since* I'm keeping Wags, if I refuse the date, I'm basically turning down Ford publicly. Even if everyone in Rush Creek couldn't put two and two together, Nan would help them."

Sonya shakes her head. "I wouldn't think of it as lose-lose. Spending a night at a fun festival with a very hot firefighter doesn't seem like a losing situation to me."

I sigh. Wags sighs, too.

"Ladies?" Carol calls to us. "I don't want to rush you, but I have a couple of phone calls I need to make—"

"We're good," I call back. I return to the desk and hold out my hand. Carol smiles and deposits the *Ford Plus One* ticket in my open palm.

Sonya very wisely doesn't say anything.

We leave, with Wags's leash in my hand and the ticket in my pocket.

Because maybe I want Sonya to be right. Maybe *wanting to* is a good enough reason. Maybe letting myself want—and have—*is* self-care.

And despite everything I said to Sonya, despite my protests and fears and... well, all the baggage and shit...

It's not too often a guy like that storms through your front door, all sexy command, and then slips back out again with a twinkle. And I'd like a second chance to make a first impression.

4

FORD

The day of the Hott & Cold Festival, I pick Reggie up in my truck.

The shelter had texted me to tell me Reggie had adopted Wags and claimed my plus-one ticket. When I saw the text, I fist pumped. As pissed as I was at Nan for her interference, I couldn't complain about the outcome.

The shelter gave me Reggie's phone number, which she had left with them and said they could pass along, so I texted her to say, *hey*.

She texted right back, *hey*.

Wasn't trying to trick you into going out with me, I tapped out. *I think Nan had an agenda.*

Long silence. Then, *Well, it worked.* She added a tongue-out winky emoji.

I blew out a breath of relief. *Pick you up at 1:15 Sat?*

Sounds good, she texted in reply.

It isn't wild enthusiasm, but I can work with it. I have a whole afternoon to show her how good things can be between us.

When I pull up at her place, she's standing in the snowy building parking lot with Wags at her side. The event welcomes all leashed, well-behaved dogs, and having experienced a long photo shoot with Wags as my partner, I can definitely verify that he's easygoing.

Reggie looks beautiful. Her hair is down, and the colors are vivid, like she touched them up since I saw her last. Her cheeks are pink, her lips cherry red, her eye makeup thick and dark. The night of the fire, she must have taken her makeup off, so I know her eyelashes are pale... but even without lipstick, her lips were lush and pink and lickable.

I had to work hard not to think about kissing her the whole time I was lecturing about candle safety. That would have been unprofessional.

She wears a black coat that looks like something Morticia Addams would favor—calf length, fitted to her curvy figure, with poofs of fabric at the shoulders and a curved diagonal row of snaps up the front. Under it, I can just see black tights and black combat boots. No hat, no gloves.

"Aren't you going to be cold?" I ask her.

"Don't do that thing," she says. "The thing where you're all protective. I can decide my own temperature."

I bite back a smile as she climbs up into the truck.

If you'd told me the woman who would mess up my head more than anyone has in years would be angry and dressed in all black, I would have laughed my ass off, but here she is.

We drive up to the Hott property, making awkward small talk about how our weeks have gone (hers: long but good;

mine: there was a fire at the Goodall ranch; no one was hurt but the hay barn burned). The festival is being held in the big area between the wedding barn, the lodge, and the ranch house.

I circle the truck and hold out my hand. She eyes it suspiciously but grasps it and hops down. I don't let her go when she lands. "This okay?" I say, instead, and she bites her lip and says, "I guess."

"You *guess*," I tease. "I can let go if you don't like it."

"No, it's fine. Your hand's warm." She gives me a shy sidelong look, and it feels like a big win.

We walk side by side toward the crowds. There are kids and dogs everywhere, the kids in a frenzy of excitement over a candy cane hunt in progress. Couples hand-in-hand sip from to-go cups of cocoa. There's a pop-up skating rink, a snow maze, sleigh rides, a big stage. A gigantic banner over the stage proclaims that dogs eager for adoption will be introduced on the hour and half hour. But right now, it's ten past and—

"Are those dogs dancing?" I ask incredulously.

"Oh, yeah," Reggie says. "That's Sonya's stepmom's thing. Haven't you seen them yet?"

"No. But they're—very talented."

They are—they boogey in time to the music, getting up on their hind legs and moving their forelegs in surprisingly human ways. I stare for a while.

"Wow," I say, turning to her to see if she's as impressed by the spectacle as I am. But she's not looking at the stage. Her attention's on a couple on the other side of the audience.

My eyes follow hers. It's a tall sandy-haired man

holding the hand of a black-haired woman with her locks twisted in a bun.

"Reggie?"

Her gaze snaps to mine, but something's gone from it, some light, and she pulls her hand out of mine. I hate the chill that slips into my palm where her heat was a moment ago, but I hate the blankness in her expression more.

"Everything okay?"

"Yeah, fine," she says, but I can tell she's full of it.

"Who are they?"

At first I think she's not going to answer. Then she sighs and says, "It's my ex-husband, Hardy, and his new girl-friend. Twenty-four year old dance teacher."

Ouch.

I don't say it out loud, but I must wince visibly, because she says, "Yeah. I'm mostly over it. I just wasn't expecting to see them. I thought they were in Santorini."

"Santorini, huh? The Greek island? So, your ex-cliché ran off with his new cliché to a cliché?"

She snorts a laugh, the color coming back into her face, and it's like that feeling when you fill in the last square of a puzzle. The world clicking into place.

Just then the blond guy looks up, his attention sliding our way. His eyes flicker with recognition when he catches sight of Reggie, and I can't help myself: I reach out and tug her close, settling an arm around her. She gives me a quick, startled look. I shrug and smile.

We both look over at her ex and his cliché. The blond guy's mouth falls open.

Reggie's smile peeks out of hiding, faint, like early spring flowers, promising summer and stirring my blood.

Hardy and his girlfriend move off.

Reggie looks up at me, her eyes a vivid July-sky blue with lighter flecks and a darker ring around the outside. They're beautiful.

"Well," she says. "That coulda gone way worse, I guess."

I raise an eyebrow. "What, like he could have tried to introduce you to her?"

"I've met her," she says, biting her lip. "I took her yoga class with him once."

We both wince this time.

She shakes her head, her mouth wry. "I just mean, if I had to see him at all, I'm at least glad I look good and I'm on a date with a hot firefighter. Even if it's a fundraiser. He doesn't have to know that."

I need to set her straight that even though this is a fundraiser, I'm with her because I want to be. The only thing I'd change if I did it over is I'd ask her straight out if she wanted to go to the festival with me, instead of letting it happen by chance.

Although then she wouldn't have Wags, who leans his head against her thigh like he's found his happy place. (Dude, I feel you.) And I'm pretty sure she and Wags were fated to be together, regardless of what happens between Reggie and me.

I know what I hope happens.

I'm about to tell her all that when she says, "Holy crap, what is *that*?"

5

REGGIE

It's doga. Doggie yoga. No joke.

"I had no idea that even existed," I say.

Ford smiles at me, eye crinkles and perfect angle-bracket smile lines. "You want to try it?"

"Hell yes."

Ford's hand enfolds mine as he leads me toward the mats. His hand is large and warm, and it's been a long time since I was touched like this. It makes my fingertips tingle, lights up a network of nerves into a fireworks display.

I think of Sonya saying that maybe self-care is letting myself have what I want. Right now what I want is to have lots more of Ford touching me. That big warm hand other places, his mouth bossy on mine, the whole length of his body hard against me.

It feels good to want it, and even better to think about letting it happen.

Our eyes meet, and I feel like he can see my thoughts, because his eyes darken before my gaze drops.

I know he's here because I adopted Wags... but I want to believe he wants the same thing I want. That maybe Sonya's right, and the tease he dropped on my doorstep the night of the fire was an invitation.

"Grab a mat!" an instructor calls.

The last time I was in a yoga class was when I went with Hardy to his girlfriend's class... but I'm not going to let her poison something I love, and I've always loved yoga.

Ford and I take side-by-side mats, trading off turns with Wags, who is definitely a natural. I wonder if someone did doga with him before he landed in the shelter. I warm quickly in the big heated yoga tent, despite the frigid outdoor temps, and I have to strip off my coat. It's not easy doing yoga—or doga—in a mini skirt, but I don't worry too much about it, because I'm wearing thick fleece tights—basically leggings—underneath. Though downward dog feels a bit—risky. Wags is an expert, but I feel self-conscious as I raise my mini-skirted butt sky high and spread my legs.

Until I catch Ford ogling my ass from upside down, eyes dark and focused.

I wonder if we're picturing the same thing. Me sinking to my hands and knees, him crowding his big solid body behind me, his hands on my hips—

Ohhh.

I'm a little light-headed when I right myself. He looks dazed, too.

"How about a ride?" he asks.

My eyes must get huge, because his eyebrows go up.

"Sleigh ride," he says, amused, gesturing toward the line.

My face gets hot.

"Or," he says, mouth turning up even farther at the corners, "I'm happy to help out with anything else you're looking for."

I blush deeper. "I might," I whisper, "take you up on that."

When I do meet his eyes, they're blazing back at me. His hand comes to the side of my face, and my mouth opens a little in anticipation—but he only brushes my hair back behind my ear.

"Your hair is beautiful," he says.

That melts me. People tell me my hair is "cool," or "fun," or sometimes "a great statement." They don't usually say it's beautiful. And definitely not the way he said it, soft as a caress.

I'm tilting toward him a little bit. I restore myself to vertical. "Thank you," I say.

Ford's smile gets bigger, with a delicious side of male smugness that only makes me wish we weren't in a crowd.

"Cocoa?" he asks.

He buys me the largest size hot chocolate. While we stand in line for the *sleigh* ride, he wraps both my hands around the to-go cup, warming them between his and the thick paper. Standing this close, I can see the beginnings of dark shadow on his sculpted jaw, his mouth the only soft thing about his face. I can't stop looking at it.

"Reggie?" someone says behind me.

I turn to find Hanna—who owns Hott Spot salon—with her husband, Easton, and their baby, Eloise. "Oh, hey, Han," I say. "Hey, Easton. This is—"

I pause.

Ford steps in. "Ford Cartwright," he says.

"Hey, Ford," Hanna says. "It's been a while!" Meeting my curious gaze, she says, "We went to school together." She glances from Ford to me, questions in her eyes.

I know, sister; I have all the same questions.

"I won a fake date with him by adopting Wags," I say, by way of explanation.

"It's a real date," Ford says.

Hanna gives both of us a quizzical look. I can't help her, because Ford's statement caught me off guard, too.

"Um, well," she says. "Have fun with that. Easton and I are off to help judge the snowperson contest."

She gives me one last mystified look before she and Easton head off toward a jumble of icy sculptures, some of which are elaborate enough to count as art.

"You didn't have to say that," I tell him. "About it being a real date."

One corner of his mouth curves. "It *is* a real date. I want to be here with you. So assuming you want to be here with me, that makes it a real date."

My stomach goes warm. "Yeah. I, uh, do."

The curve of his mouth blossoms into a full-blown smile. "Good."

"You two!" the sleigh driver instructs, and it's our turn to climb into the sleigh. The portable wooden steps are steep, and Ford takes my hand again, Wags jumping up. We sit side by side in the sleigh, Wags settling on the seat beside me, Ford's arm draped around me. I lean into him, pulled like a magnet. He's sturdy and warm, and I can feel all the muscle through our clothes. The thickness of his biceps, the cords in his forearm, the bunching and stretching through his side. Something settles, warm and liquid, in my low belly.

The horses pull us around the perimeter of Hanna's family's ranchland, now the site of the Hott Springs Eternal wedding venue. Everything is snow covered, muted and lovely.

We chat about nothing for a bit. His crewmates, my coworkers at the salon. How we spent winters as kids—him, in Rush Creek, building snow forts and having snowball fights and ice skating on the lakes and ponds. Skiing at Mt. Bachelor. Me, in Ohio, doing essentially the same thing, minus the skiing. Minus the mountains.

We both stare out at the Cascades, standing in the distance, mostly white-capped at this time of year. Beautiful, remote, and ragged.

"Sometimes I look at them and just feel like everything's going to be OK. Like they've been standing so long, and nothing can faze them," Ford says.

"Well, except volcanoes," I point out.

He snorts. "Thanks, sunshine."

"Just telling it like it is."

"'The boobs are real. The smile is fake.'"

"Exactly," I say, pleased that he remembers. And then not so pleased, because I suddenly recall that I don't want him to relive that night. But it's too late. I bite my lip and say, "Can you just forget what you saw that night? Pretend it didn't happen?"

Ford blinks. Frowns. "What if—" He stops. "What if I don't *want* to forget what I saw that night?"

Our eyes meet. His are dark and intent.

I bite my lip. "You don't?"

He shakes his head. "No. I *liked* what I saw. Or what I imagined I was seeing," he amends, the corners of his mouth curving.

I blush fiercely.

His eyes rake over the blush, deepening it. "Yeah. That's what I thought," he murmurs.

I can't look away from the challenge in his gaze, my body riding anticipation so sharp it's almost pain.

With an abrupt jolt, the sleigh ride ends and our fellow passengers start disembarking.

I stand, but before I can extricate myself from the sleigh, he stands and scoops me up. I gasp, laughing, struggling.

"Put me down!" I cry.

Chuckling, he ignores me. He hops down the temp steps and jogs with me in his arms, Wags panting along behind us.

I don't let him see how much I like that. I turn my face into his chest. He smells like snow and cold, a whiff of smoke. I could lick him.

"Put me down," I say, with way less conviction.

"Nope," he says, still trotting with me in his arms, into a small grove of trees, out of view. Wags follows us into a clearing. It's a winter wonderland, the branches coated with a thin sparkle of snow and ice, the sky bright blue above our heads. A wooden bench squats at one side of the clearing, iced over from a recent storm.

"How did you know this was here?" I ask, drinking in the beauty of the scene as he sets me on my feet.

"I played in these woods with the Hott brothers, growing up." He watches me quietly as Wags settles at our feet, lying down and closing his eyes. Ford takes both my hands again, his big and warm and swallowing mine up... and the intensity of his gaze scares me.

No, that's not what scares me.

What scares me is how good it feels. How much I like it. How much I want this—Ford and me—to be happening.

"So," he says, voice low and thick with suggestion. My core softens in anticipation. "That night. In the tub. I've been wondering."

He lets go of one of my hands. Reaches out. Rubs his thumb over my lip.

"Did you finish?"

His eyes are dark, serious. I can't look away. I don't want to look away. My mouth is so dry, I don't trust myself to speak. Instead, I shake my head.

"I didn't think so," he says roughly. "I was pretty sure you got interrupted. And you know what I really wanted to do that night?" His thumb slides over my lip, tugging it down, slicking across the sensitive inner curve, and my whole body goes liquid. "I wanted to pick you up and carry you back to that bedroom and lay you down. Tell you I knew exactly what you were doing in the bathtub and ask if you'd let me get you there."

A helpless whimper breaks from my lips, and heat flashes into his eyes. I have no more than a second to love it, the fire, the need, and then his mouth is on mine, replacing his thumb. Hard, hungry, completely in control. His hand fits behind my head; his body presses along the length of mine, and I moan softly again. He makes a soft broken sound deep in his chest, almost a growl, and the kiss deepens, his tongue finding mine, sending pleasure to every nerve ending in my skin. His mouth slides away, trailing kisses along my jaw, down my throat. Ford unsnaps my coat and tugs it open, his lips moving into the scoop of my black lace top, finding the curve of my breast.

"I've been thinking about doing this," he breathes. "Getting you off."

My body goes molten at his words.

He pulls my top down, finds the lace edge of my bra, peels that away, too, his mouth following the path he's cleared for himself to my nipple, which he takes in his mouth. The contrast between the icy air on my skin and the heat of his mouth and hands winds me up, and up. His mouth is tight on my nipple, insistent. My breasts, always sensitive, are on fire for him, the deep tug between nipples and clit bright and alive, bringing me close enough that I wonder if he could send me over the edge this way.

His big hand slides down my front, cupping between my legs; I press into it, tipping my hips, reaching for more. And then I have a moment of sanity, clarity:

"Someone might see us."

"That's true," he murmurs, his breath a warm brush against my ear. "So I'll just have to make you come fast."

One more hungry kiss that doesn't end, one more pinch of my nipple, his fingers flicking over it afterwards to caress away the almost-pain, one more tight, hard rock of his big palm over the aching place between my legs, and I'm there, coming for him, coming so hard for him. His mouth muffling my cries and his hands slowing so he can soothe me back down.

And no one sees, and the snow muffles sound enough that I can tell myself no one heard, either. And while it's possible I'm wrong about that, I honestly can't even bring myself to feel bad about it.

6

FORD

She stumbles to the bench and sits down. She laughs when her butt touches the ice, and murmurs, "It feels good. I'm so hot and swollen; the cold feels good. God. Everything feels good."

I smile at her. I've been wanting to do that for a while now, and the satisfaction on her face is as rewarding for me as the thrill of a well-executed rescue.

"C'mere," she says.

I do, stepping between her legs.

"It's cold," she warns.

"I can handle it," I tell her.

She unzips me, and before I can take the full force of the ice-cold air, she lowers her mouth to me.

"*Fuck*," I whisper. "You don't have to—"

"Shh," she says around me, and her tongue is a thing of beauty, strong and limber and everywhere at once, the stud cold in contrast to the heat of her. I have to hold myself back so I don't thrust too deep for her, but she keeps one hand on my ass and one on the front of my thigh, showing me, setting the depth, and I move against the caress of her mouth.

"You're so fucking hot. God. That's so good."

She groans her approval against my swollen, needy cock.

Holding back, not thrusting into her mouth, is its own pleasure. I don't let myself push, so the tension builds and winds at the base of my spine.

"Reggie—"

"Shh, it's okay," she says again, and then I'm coming against the soft rub and hard stud of her tongue, my hand tangling deep in her hair.

"Fuck," I say, when she lets me go, smiling, and zips me back up.

Wags opens one eye, then the other, lifts his head from the icy floor. Staggers to his feet and leans his nose against Reggie's knee.

"Hey, bud," she says. "Thanks for sleeping through that."

She stands up and I open my arms. She steps into them, leaning her head against my shoulder. We're cuddling, I realize. I'm surprised and also not surprised to find out she's a cuddler. I cup her head, stroking her hair. "Thank you," I say quietly, and she tips her face up and smiles at me.

I smile back.

When both of our legs are a little less wobbly, we head out of our little snow cul-de-sac with Wags trailing.

I'm grinning, a whisper away from whistling. But the festival's just about over, and I don't want the day to end.

"How would you feel about coming back here with me tonight to the Hott & Cold Holiday Prom?" I ask her.

I'm watching her face, so I clock the moment it freezes. The moment when she steps back out of my embrace, the side of my body going cold.

"Ford," she says. "You don't have to do that."

"It's not a have to," I say, my stomach going cold. I knew we should have addressed the issue of the fake versus real date sooner. "I want to. Reggie, I know this started out as a fundraiser, but I like you. I really, really like you. And I want to spend more time with you."

She won't meet my eyes.

"Reggie."

"I can't," she says. "I'm not... ready."

It's an echo of her words at the salon, of Nan's assertion that if I asked Reggie straight out, she'd turn me down. The only reason this day has happened at all is because it was always pretend in her mind.

She sighs. "Ford... I've had a really good time today, but I think we should call it quits now. Before—before anyone gets hurt." She closes her eyes. "I mean, that night was pretty emblematic. What you saw that night was who I am right now. My therapist told me I should try to practice some... *self care*."

The last two words are forced out against the backdrop of a deep blush.

"And you saw how well *that* went. I'm a hot mess. And I don't want to put that on you, or anyone else. I need some time to be, I don't know, more... more *solid*."

I'm trying to find the right words around the ball of emotions in my chest, and they're not coming. She grasps

Wags's leash and says, "In other words, this is a classic example of 'it's not you, it's me.' But in this case, it's really true."

"Reggie," I say.

"Please don't," she says. "Let's just agree it was an amazing day."

She gives me a quick fierce hug, and the feel of her body against mine steals all my words.

"I can get a ride home with Sonya," she says.

And then she's walking away from me, and I'm left feeling like she's kicked me in the ribs.

It's weirdly familiar, and then I get it: It's the sensation of being kicked as someone struggles when you're trying to save them.

I'm not saying I'm rescuing Reggie. Fuck no. If there's anyone capable of taking care of herself, it's this woman.

I'm just saying sometimes you take a kick in the ribs and keep trying because you know something good and right will come out of it.

"Reggie," I say. "Stop. Just stop for a fucking second, and let me tell you something."

REGGIE

I stop, because Ford's command has so much authority. It's not the kind of tone you ignore... and plus, I can feel it between my legs, a rumble of pleasure.

I turn around, and he's standing there, arms crossed, not so different from how he looked when he showed up at my house. Less gear. Same expression on his face.

"You say you were a hot mess that night." He shakes his head. "That's not what I saw."

"No?"

"No. I saw a woman who knows what she needs and how to get it."

My reaction must show on my face, because he laughs and shakes his head. "That, yeah—I mean, of course. It was a total thirst trap, seeing what you'd been up to, and it gave me all kinds of ideas. We've already been over that. And—" He gives me a long, assessing look. "I'm not done with those ideas, by the way.

My body goes hot again.

"But that's not what I mean. I mean that you weren't counting on anyone else to help you figure out who you were and what worked for you—that's the part that I liked."

Now it's the ache in my chest that has my attention right now, the feeling that the ice there wants to crack, wants to melt, but I won't, can't let it, because...

Because I'm too scared.

"And I saw a woman who's got a head on her shoulders in an emergency. Who put out a fire, who did what needed to be done. Smart, calm, with it. Not a hot mess at all. Grace under pressure."

His eyes are steady on mine, and all I can think about is Sonya saying, *Maybe self care is letting yourself have what you know you want.*

"I saw a woman with a t-shirt that cracked me up. A dick candle altar on the bedside table. A sense of humor. *My* sense of humor. I wanted to laugh. I wanted to know you better. And I was totally right, because every little bit I've gotten to know you today has only made me want to know you more. Better. All the way."

Tears press at the backs of my eyes, threatening in a way they haven't, not once, since Hardy left.

"You weren't supposed to see any of that," I tell him, finally finding my words. "You weren't supposed to know any of that."

"I get that," he says. "But I did. I saw you sweaty and flustered and off your game. Alone and trying to make the most of it. And I wanted more of you."

It feels like he's taking a blowtorch to the ice in my chest—too much at once, but also the only way back to myself.

"I don't want you to be disappointed," I confess.

He just stares at me, like the words I'm saying don't make any sense.

"Like Hardy was, in the end," I explain, and my voice cracks on it. My eyes fill with tears.

And then they're spilling down my face, and he takes a step closer, cupping my face in his hand and swiping the tears away with calloused thumbs. Lowering his mouth to mine and kissing me in a way that feels like the connection I was craving, like an asked and answered question.

"Reggie," he murmurs. "I will never be disappointed."

"You can't know that. Hardy must have thought that, too, at first."

"Hardy is a complete and total fool. He obviously had no idea what to do with a real woman or how to hang onto a good thing. His loss is my gain, and I'm not the kind of guy who will ever forget that."

And that's it. The ice melts, and I'm breathless, drowning in the sensation.

Then I find air, and my voice.

"I like you, too," I say. "I've liked you since you showed up at my house and oozed confidence and competence and rescued me—"

"You rescued yourself," he reminds me, but a smile has broken out on his face, laugh crinkles forming.

"You did tell me how to clean up the yucky fire extinguisher mess."

He raises his eyebrows, laughter in his eyes. "You could have looked that up on Google."

"You made me feel like things were going to be okay," I say. "And I loved being with you today. And what we did. In the woods. I want to—I want to do that again. But first... I want to go to holiday prom."

A grin blooms on his face, full flower. "Yeah?" he says.

"Yeah."

"Yes!" He pumps his fist and makes me laugh.

I look at my phone. "Give me an hour."

CHAPTER 8

FORD

Reggie gets a ride home with Sonya, and true to our agreement, I arrive at her place an hour later. I leave the car in her apartment building's parking area, and climb the steps to her place, knocking at the door.

The door opens, and Reggie stands there, and holy shit.

She's wearing a short black dress sewn from several layers of lace. It's feminine AF but also incredibly badass, like Reggie. The heart-shaped neckline makes her already amazing tits look like a feast set out for me, deliciously pale against the black fabric. She's wearing black cat-eye liner and mascara and a whole bunch of other eye makeup. Red lipstick. I want to kiss it off right fucking now. And that's before I see the combat boots.

"You look incredible," I tell her.

She smiles at me. "So do you."

"Those boots," I say. "You can keep them on later when I take the rest of it off."

"I was planning on it," she says, and her smile gets bigger.

"Reggie," I say roughly, and then we're kissing, soft mouth and hard stud, and it's all I can do to take my hands off her and get us out the door so we don't miss holiday prom completely.

The Hott & Cold Holiday Prom is in full swing when we arrive, vibrant with red and green dresses and matching cummerbunds. A huge Christmas tree squats in the corner, decked out in colored lights and an eclectic collection of ornaments. The room, darkened for dancing, sparkles with the reflections off a disco ball.

We take a minute to absorb the atmosphere. At the front of the room, a DJ spins a mix of '80s hits and holiday songs from every decade. People dance in groups and pairs, a happy fray. I spot Sonya and her boyfriend, Hanna and her husband, an assortment of my crewmates with the dates who won them by adopting dogs. The expressions on their faces are pretty hilarious, ranging from "how the hell did I get myself into this" to "how the hell do I get myself out of this?"

And then, of course, there's me. Holy shit, I lucked out. I slide a look sideways at Reggie, at the rare smile on her face and the curves of her body under that black dress. I'm a huge fan. Though that doesn't stop me from thinking about later, when I'll be removing that black dress from her killer curves and running my hands over every inch of her. When I'll be following my fingertips with my lips and tongue until she cries out my name.

When the thick heels of those boots will be digging into my ass.

As if she can hear my thoughts, she looks up and gives

me a knowing smile, then slips her hand into mine. It's trusting, confiding, and I squeeze her hand back, so grateful to be here with the most beautiful woman in the room, to have earned her willingness to give this thing between us a shot.

"Into the Groove" comes on, and Reggie beams and tugs me onto the dance floor. She's a good dancer, sexy and uninhibited, and I watch her with frank interest. She holds my gaze, sending a little challenge back at me. *You like?* her expression seems to say, and as I swing into motion across from her, I let everything in my eyes and face tell her *hell yes*. Heat surges between us, as we dance, holding eye contact. Her eyes are dark with need, her lower lip soft enough to make me think of the sensation of her mouth on my dick.

The music shifts, Coldplay's version of "Have Yourself a Merry Little Christmas." I hold out my arms, and she doesn't hesitate before stepping into them. She's soft and curvy to the touch, and she settles her cheek against my shoulder. It feels like she's meant to be there, and my heart pounds with the pure pleasure of it. The rightness of it.

We slow dance to the song, our bodies drifting closer and closer together. The space between us feels supercharged with chemistry, and I can't help the way blood swells my cock. She apparently doesn't mind, because she nudges her hip against my erection, then tilts her chin to smirk up at me.

"Yeah," I say. "That's what you do to me."

"You're good for my ego."

"The big guy doesn't lie."

She cracks up. "Seriously, Ford? *The big guy doesn't lie?*"

But I just pull her closer and lower my face to rest my cheek against her hair. It's soft and silky and smells like spring rain and roses. I like the contradictions—Reggie, dressed all in black, wearing combat boots, and smelling like flowers and the gentlest season.

It's possible we would have found our way to each other even if she hadn't set her bedskirt on fire, but I can't help feeling like this was meant to be.

"Do you believe in fate?" I ask her.

She shrugs. "Not really."

"I feel like either I have to believe in fate, or think that the Roomba was programmed by Nan."

She hoots a laugh. "I wouldn't put it past her."

The song ends and "Sweet Dreams (Are Made of This)" starts up. But I don't let Reggie go, and she doesn't try to get away. We just stand there, holding each other, enjoying the moment.

A flash of bright pink snares both our eyes; it's Nan in a dress so vivid it's practically fluorescent. She's dancing with my crewmate, her grandson. She lifts her head and catches my eye, raising an eyebrow when she spots me still holding Reggie. *See?* she mouths.

Thank you, I tell her, and she beams.

"I think we made Nan's holiday season," I tell Reggie.

"Good," she says, reaching up to stroke the soft edge Mei cut into my hair. Her touch feels electric, delicious. "Because she made mine."

Everyone around us is dancing and we're standing still in each other's arms.

"I've changed my mind," Reggie says. She steps back

and crosses her arms, smirking a little. "About being at holiday prom with you."

I raise my eyebrows.

Her eyes twinkle as she looks up at me, bright as Christmas lights. "I'd way rather be home in bed with you."

I scoop her up, throw her over my shoulder, and carry her out.

As much as I loved holding her in my arms and dancing with her, this is the moment I've been waiting for. I open the door to my apartment, and watch her face as she sees what I've done.

There's a trail of white twinkly lights leading up my stairs, and she turns to look at me, amusement and wonder on her face.

"What did you do?" she asks.

"I had an hour," I say. "It doesn't take me an hour to put on a tux."

That makes her laugh.

I nod my head to indicate that she should follow the lights, and she does, climbing the stairs with me right behind her, admiring her bare creamy thighs, unable to stop myself from reaching out and running a finger from the inside of her knee upward. I hear her soft exhalation, and it makes me instantly hard. She looks back at me with a knowing grin, and I raise my eyebrow as if to say *yup*.

The lights lead her up to my bedroom, where they ring the bed.

"No candles," I say. "Safer."

She snorts.

"C'mon," I say, and lead her along the last little bit of lit path into the bathroom.

"Self care," I say, gesturing. "I have a very adjustable removable shower nozzle. I myself use it mainly for getting soap off my back, but I hear rumors it's good for other things. You could show me. Or I could show you. Whichever you'd rather."

Her eyes are big, her lower lip soft and full and a little wet. I want to lick it. I want to lick all of her.

I turn on the water in the tub and spin her around to give me access to the zipper on her dress. I unzip it and let it fall to the bathroom floor, leaving her in just a black lace bra and matching panties. This time it's my exhalation that's audible in the quiet space, and she turns in my arms and slides close.

Then she pulls back just a bit and gives me a wicked smile. "Where's my dick candle?" she asks.

I burst out laughing. Then I sober.

"I have something *way* better for you," I tell her.

Then I proceed to give her exactly what she wants for Christmas.

Love Reggie? She first appeared in *Hott Shot*, the first book in my Hott Springs Eternal series. Want to hear what happens when gruff Quinn gets forced to be the receptionist for sunny Sonya's beloved Hott Spot Spa? Hint: grumpy-sunshine, sparks-flying hilarious deliciousness! Grab *Hott Shot* now!

Go to geni.us/HottShot

Keep reading for an excerpt from *Hott Shot*!

EXCERPT FROM HOTT SHOT
QUINN

As a scientist, I'm used to predicting outcomes, taking every variable into account. But sitting with my siblings around the big conference table in the lawyer's office, reading my late grandfather's letter, I'm not a scientist at all. I'm just a sucker-punched guy—and there's *no* way I could have seen this coming.

Okay, Quinn. You think you're such a hot shot? Let's see how you handle a completely different kind of business.

I look up to find my sibs staring at me with expressions ranging from total confusion to barely veiled amusement.

"What does that mean?" my brother Rhys demands.

My brother Preston shakes his head in disgust. "It means the man couldn't help himself. He can't let death stop him from making trouble. What a total dick move."

"Language," the lawyer chides. "There are ladies present."

Arthur Weggers is my granddad's attorney. He's a short, balding, sixty-something guy with pasty skin who I had no reason to dislike before today but who I would happily donate to science right now.

"This woman doesn't give a fuck," my sister, Hanna—eight months pregnant and sporting a watermelon front and center—says with a shrug.

"Keep reading," the lawyer urges.

But I've had enough. I thrust the letter back into Weggers's hands. "He can't do this."

"He can," Weggers says. "We've been over this, Quinn. He made sure the will was airtight. He had two different medical professionals attest to his soundness of mind and body. He had me review the no-contest clause with three other lawyers."

Rhys, who's also an attorney, mutters something next to me.

"What's that?" Weggers says.

"Deadhand control," my brother repeats louder.

The two men glare at each other across the table.

Rhys turns to us. "It's what it sounds like. Most states won't let people just keep exerting infinite control after they're dead."

Weggers scowls. "If you'd like to take a shot at contesting the will, that is, of *course*, your prerogative."

Rhys scowls back. "Believe me. I'm looking into it."

He's taking this will extremely personally.

But not as personally as I'm taking it.

My granddad's will leaves the ranchland we grew up on to the six of us: Hanna, me, and our four brothers. But it also contains what Weggers calls *conditions* and I call the Asshole Clause. We have to hold the land for two years before we can sell it, and during those two years, we have to comply with any "additional instructions" my grandfather provides.

"What does he mean, 'additional instructions'?" Preston demanded when Weggers first read that clause to us, two days ago, after all of us had been summoned back to Rush Creek for the funeral. "It's not like he's around to tell us what to do."

"I'm afraid I can't say more," Weggers said, loftily. "It will make more sense *in time*."

He deposited those words into the air like a television chef sprinkling finishing salt—the first moment when it became clear he wasn't on our side.

Today, apparently, is "in time." Weggers summoned us with a group text: *Your first instruction is to appear in my office at 5 p.m. on the day following your grandfather's burial.*

When we were assembled, he handed me a letter-sized envelope containing a single sheet of paper, typed and signed in my grandfather's arthritic lifelong rancher's hand. "Read it out loud," Weggers said.

"I'd rather read it to myself first."

He shook his head. "Out loud."

It's like my granddad is speaking through a pushy, bald medium. Weggers just needs a crystal ball and some patter about the spirits from beyond, and he could be a fortune teller in a back-alley tent.

Now he pushes the sheet of paper back into my hands. "Go on."

I continue reading from where I left off:

You'll work as the Hott Springs Eternal spa and salon recep-

tionist for sixty days, starting no later than forty-eight hours from the date of this letter. The spa is open six days a week from 10 to 6; you'll sit at the front desk for those hours, minus a thirty-minute lunch break. You'll live in Hott Springs staff housing for the duration of your duties. And lest you think this is an opportunity to phone it in, the spa must operate profitably during your tenure, *without your personal financial contribution.*

The numbers swim in front of my eyes, so it takes a minute for the full meaning to sink in. Receptionist. Front desk.

People. Polite small talk. All day long.

Way to hit me when I'm down, Granddad.

I close my eyes, half hoping that when I open them again, this will all be a bad dream.

"It doesn't have to be Quinn, does it?" Preston asks. "One of us could do it. This is so not Quinn's thing."

He's right about that. I think of Freya's words to me: *I'm a people person, and you're a things-and-ideas person. It would never have worked long term.*

Those words hurt like hell when she delivered them, but she was only telling me what other people in my life had already taught me. Better to know your limits, right?

I give Preston a half nod of thanks.

"It has to be Quinn," Weggers says. "Your grandfather is very clear that the instructions have to be followed to a *T*. We'll set up a webcam so I can check on Quinn periodically to make sure he's fulfilling the terms."

"You'll—what?" Rhys's mouth hangs open.

"As your grandfather's lawyer *and* his executor, it's my job to make sure the conditions get met."

"And if the conditions *don't* get met?" Rhys asks.

"Then the land passes to Blue Iron Mining."

"Are you—are you *shitting* us?" Preston demands. "Why the hell would he...?"

But he trails off because the answer's obvious. Even though we don't want to live on the land, Granddad knew exactly how much we'd hate the idea of stripping it for profit.

Just like that, I get it. I understand my grandfather's game. And I think my brothers do, too, because when I look up, they're all looking back at me with alarm on their faces.

"We're next," Preston says. "Aren't we? Because he couldn't get us back to Rush Creek any other way, he decided to do it from beyond the grave. If he's gonna do this to Quinn, he's gonna do it to all of us." He turns to Weggers. "He's got some equally evil scheme up his sleeve for each of us. Doesn't he?"

Weggers smiles, mean and pleased. "I'm afraid I can't say. Your grandfather was quite clear that all this happens on a need-to-know basis."

This guy is enjoying himself way too much.

"Look," I say, trying to calm myself down because throwing a temper tantrum won't get me anywhere. "I can see he's trying to make a point. Forcing me back to Rush Creek. Humbling me or whatever."

Because the letter echoes the fight my grandfather and I had when I finally told him that, like my older brothers, I wasn't coming back to Rush Creek to run the ranch.

C'mon, Quinn. If you can establish a multibillion-dollar biotech company, surely you can handle this job.

Unless you can't.

From beyond the grave, my granddad is still trying to best me at a game I never agreed to play.

"Did you know about this?" Preston asks Hanna. Not accusing, exactly, but wary.

She's pale when we all turn to look at her, her skin even lighter than usual against the backdrop of her short, nearly black hair. "No. God, no. Swear I didn't. I knew he had something up his sleeve after none of you guys showed up for his eighty-fifth birthday party, but then when no evil plan materialized in the last two years, I thought..." She closes her eyes. "I underestimated him. Or overestimated him."

There's a collective sigh of relief. Hanna's constitutionally incapable of lying, and we all know it. None of us wanted to believe she would've let this happen, but it's still a relief to know she didn't.

Because...Jesus, what a mind fuck.

My brain jumps around, trying to find a way out, but there isn't one—not that I can see.

This isn't like jury duty. I can't claim that I'm so essential elsewhere that I'm exempt. And truthfully, now's not the worst time to take a break from my company, MedThena.

But that doesn't mean I belong at Hott Spot, either. Especially not if it means taking someone else's place.

"I can't steal a receptionist's job," I say.

For a moment, this freezes Weggers. Apparently he's not such a dick that he can take pleasure in someone losing their job over my grandfather's twisted joke.

Hanna coughs. We all turn to look at her.

"Actually, our receptionist hasn't shown up for the last five days," she says quietly, rubbing her temple as if her head hurts. "We're not sure what's up with her. The staff's been filling in till we sort it out—but it would be great to have you there. And if she does come back, we could always have her work up at the main resort desk. There's going to be plenty of work with me heading into maternity leave."

She sounds weary, and for the first time, I register that her exhaustion isn't just grief. My sister has always been the strongest, healthiest person I know, but right now? She looks like someone wrung her out. A knot forms behind my rib cage. My brothers are right: I'm not a people person. And I've been a bad brother. But holy God, I love my sister. As a kid, she was a stubborn, often-angry spark plug of a tiny human who drove us halfway to distraction, but growing up in Rush Creek wouldn't have been the same without her.

God, I wish we'd done better by her. I flick a look at Preston, wondering if he feels any guilt for the chain reaction he started when he left Rush Creek, but he's staring at his phone. Of course he is. Preston's always working.

Hanna sighs. "I've been trying to help out up at the spa where I can, since everyone's filling in at the reception desk."

"On top of all her other jobs," says a voice from the doorway. Easton, her husband, leans there, handsome, well dressed, and usually easy going, but his expression at the moment is anything but.

"Easton, please, not right now," Hanna says.

"They need to know. They need to know how it is for

you. How you took care of your granddad. How hard you work."

Hanna presses her fingers to her forehead, wincing.

Easton's at her side instantly. "Is the headache back?" he demands.

"Yes, but—" She leans down, groaning. "God."

"What? What is it?"

She's gray.

Something turns over in my brain, an alarm signal. I'm not a doctor, but I spend an absurd amount of time in medical offices and hospitals, and I've read every warning poster so many times they're engraved on my soul.

Hanna moans. "Ow," she says, cradling her head in her hands.

"For fuck's sake," I say, panic kicking into high gear. "Call 911."

"You shoulda said something," I growl at Hanna.

She's sitting up in her hospital bed, looking immensely pregnant and very tired but much less gray and woozy. It's a huge relief to see her more or less herself again. They're letting us in to see her—but only one at a time, to keep her stress levels down. I think it's a good choice: Five Hott brothers at one time would send anyone's blood pressure through the ceiling. Having spent several hours with the four others in the waiting room, pacing like caged wolves, I'm qualified to speak to this.

"Quinn," she says, smiling at me. "You were worried, huh?"

I don't answer; we both know I was, and we both know I won't say so. Instead, I sit down in the chair next to the bed. And then, unable to help myself, I bend my head down to her belly and rest my cheek against the curve of it, above where the fetal monitor is sending a steady heartbeat to one of the machines at her bedside.

I sit up to find her giving me a hard but sympathetic look.

"Give me your hand," she commands. "She's turning somersaults."

She takes my hand with her IV-free one and clasps it to her abdomen. As soon as she does, I feel her belly give a seismic roll, almost a bounce. And holy shit. There's a person in there.

Of course, I knew there was, but experiencing it first-hand is still deeply pleasing, the way all confirmation of hypothesis is. That's part of why I love science so much.

My eyes prickle, and I pull my hand away.

"She's fine, Quinny." Her voice is tender, which is surprising because Hanna is one of the most sarcastic people I know. She's also the only person who calls me Quinny—the only person on earth I'd allow to do it.

"I've been a bad brother."

She sighs. "Not the worst. You sent me a wedding present."

"I should have been there." The wedding was eighteen months ago. Only Tucker and Shane were there, the rest of us mired in work, convinced we were too busy to make the trip. A decision I now wish I could take back.

"You send Christmas presents."

I whisper, "My assistant sends Christmas presents."

She smiles. "Because you tell her to."

I close my eyes tight. "I told her once, and she made it a repeating item in her calendar."

"You're too honest. You could've just taken the compliment."

"I couldn't. You know I couldn't." Because in a lot of ways, Hanna and I are two peas. Blunt, unpolished, gruff, prone to saying the wrong thing at the wrong time, not great at showing love. All the Hotts are a bit that way—but Hanna and I are the king and queen.

"I know," she admits, shaking her head and laughing.

Jesus, I've missed her. And I meant what I said: I've been a bad brother.

"May I?"

I hold my hand out again in the direction of her belly. She takes it and positions it over the pitch and roll of my niece.

"You're such a softie." She says it very quietly, like she knows I wouldn't want anyone to overhear.

"I'm not."

"You need to let more people see this side of you."

I shake my head because I gave that a shot with Freya, and it didn't work out so well.

"This is what you and I do. We assume people don't like us. But what I'm learning is that sometimes it's *us*, building walls so we don't get hurt like we did when we were kids. You have to take it on faith that they *do* like you and proceed accordingly."

I squint at her. "That feels like a bad bet."

She gives me a sharp look.

"Unscientific," I add.

She shrugs. "People aren't very science-y."

We're quiet for a minute. Then she says, "You don't have to do it, you know."

"Do...?"

"What Grandfather said in the will. I'll be fine, no matter what. I was fine before—working for the Wilders."

"But you love this more—working at Hott Springs Eternal."

"Yes," she says. "I do. I love it because Granddad and I did it together..."

Grief streaks across her face. She loved our grandfather. She saw a heart of gold under his crusty, manipulative surface. Part of me had hoped she was right, but the will proves she wasn't.

She collects herself because she's Hanna and growing up with five brothers taught her not to show weakness. "... and because it's on the family land, and because for the first time in my life I've built something that's—well, that's *mine*. My efforts, my results. And people come to me and tell me that I've given them a wedding weekend they won't ever forget, and—" She lifts her shoulders, palms out. "For all the reasons. But," she says, "I get it. You can't walk away from a multibillion-dollar business and come here and sit at a reception desk—that was just a fantasy Granddad had, that if he got you here, somehow..."

She trails off.

"I'd stay."

She sighs. "Yeah. I mean, I'm sure that's what he was thinking."

We don't look at each other. When Preston left, we were all in it together. But as each of my brothers shook off Rush Creek, there were fewer of us left behind. Hanna and I were the last two standing, and then...well, then I left her, too. And it's hard to forgive myself for that, especially now. Because maybe Easton's right and we let this happen to her.

"Easton's full of shit," she says, reading my mind. "This isn't your fault. Preeclampsia's a common pregnancy risk. I'm glad you guys are here, and I hope you'll stay—well, as long as you feel like you can." She runs a hand through her short hair. "But I don't want you to give up your life for me. What about MedThena?"

"I'm overdue for a vacation."

"This is more than a vacation."

"A sabbatical, then."

She's still squinting suspiciously at me.

I don't want to tell her the truth—that in the waiting room, I made a bargain with God. If Hanna was okay, if the baby was okay, I'd do...well, anything.

Even figure out how to people.

I wonder if Rhys made a similar pact with whatever being he prays to. He stopped muttering about *deadhand control* and contesting the will right around the time the doctor came into the waiting room to tell us Hanna and the baby would be okay.

"My company will be fine without me for two months," I say. "We're waiting on the results of a clinical trial."

"But will you be fine without your work?" she asks, narrowing her eyes.

Hanna's always been able to read me better than anyone else.

"Don't you worry about that."

"You don't have to fix anything. Or...atone for anything. You don't *owe* me anything.

"I'm not doing this for you," I say.

"Like hell you're not."

"You have to trust me."

She frowns. "You all used to say that when we were kids before you tied me to a tree and tickled me."

I laugh, remembering. "We were awful."

We were, like most siblings, but also...

Well. There were other times, too. The time when Rhys's new bike got stolen and we all pooled our savings to get him a new one; the time when Preston got dumped and we decided the best way to cheer him up was to subject him to a week's worth of bad pranks...

It worked, I'll add. Although we never got the ketchup out of the sheets.

Maybe she's remembering a similar moment because her grin deepens then disappears. "You don't have to do this."

I know she means it and that she'd forgive me if I turned around and went back to Boston, but that's not the point.

I think about the vow I made and broke—the first and only one. The original one. Maybe it wasn't my fault, but I still hold myself one-fifth responsible. And I will never break another one. Especially not one made on my sister's and niece's lives.

I'm still pissed as hell at my grandfather for putting me in this position. But I can do this. I don't have to be *good* at it—in fact, I might be extra bad at it, to spite my granddad. But I can still do it. For Hanna. And...the little spud.

"I do," I say. "And I will."

Want to find out what happens when grumpy Quinn goes to work at the family spa... for sunshine-y spa manager Sonya?

Go to geni.us/HottShot

PART II

WILDER FOR THE WIN

CHAPTER 1
AMANDA

I'm a woman on a mission...

...and I'm wearing an ugly Christmas sweater.

It's Santa-red with a deep, white, fur-lined scoop neck. Two knitted reindeer are parked right on my breasts, their pom-pom noses perfectly aligned with my nipples. And these tight black pants? They leave nothing to the imagination.

This outfit is just the first step in my brilliant plan to save my marriage.

I descend the stairs. Listen to make sure that Heath is actually in the kitchen. Yes, he is—I can hear him emptying the dishwasher. And there are no little voices in there with him.

Perfect.

I make my grand entrance.

Heath looks up, greets me with a nod, and returns to unloading the dishwasher—with so much concentration, you'd think he was discovering the formula for fusion.

Yeah.

It's like the sound my kids' rocket balloons make when they leave the pump and go whizzing around the room. A cross between a fart and a great big sigh of disappointment. The sound of my already punctured self-esteem, deflating.

And OK, it's not like I'm standing in the kitchen in my red lace panties, or some fabulous teddy that I bought from Frederick's of Hollywood. It's just a Christmas sweater, and yeah, it's kind of goofy. But I think I look pretty hot. I spent a long time on my makeup and my hair.

And Heath doesn't crack a smile, let alone try to tweak my pom-poms.

"Mommy Mommy Mommy Mommy!"

Three-year-old Kieran flies into the kitchen, clutching his favorite dump truck, showing me where the plastic has cracked, probably from him trying to use the dump truck and his firetruck as roller skates. He's crying.

My window of opportunity slams shut, but I am not giving up so easily. Even if I am now a Kenning, I am, by blood, a Wilder, and my five brothers and I are a stubborn bunch.

Reindeer nose nipples are only one weapon in my arsenal.

I bend to examine Kieran's wounded truck. "Oh, sorry, bud. That's super frustrating!" I kneel and give him a hug.

"Can you fix it?" he wails.

Repair-wise, I'm already in over my head. Heath knows it and steps in, taking the dump truck from my hands and nodding. "Sure, buddy," he says. "Daddies can fix everything." He opens the junk drawer and pulls out the superglue.

This is Heath in a nutshell. Emptier of dishwashers,

saver of small children's moods. He is everything I ever wanted in a husband and father.

Except that for too long now—he hasn't felt like mine. And not just because he won't tweak my pom-poms, although that's a big part of it. It's been three months, two weeks, three days, and two hours since the last time Heath and I had sex.

Yes. I'm counting.

And no, I have no idea how that happened.

But it's not just the sex. It's that other intangible piece. That feeling that we know and like each other. That we have fun together, instead of just doing what has to be done, one foot in front of the other.

These days, we're more like roommates than lovers. And I hate it.

So when I learned that Wilder Adventures, my family's business, was hosting a holiday season Winter Games & Gala?

I knew I had to take full advantage.

"Mommy!" Seven-year-old Noah runs into the kitchen. "You have pom-poms on your boobies."

See? It's not a subtle outfit. Heath has to be willfully ignoring it. I look up to see if the mention of boobies snagged his attention—but no such luck.

"Can I touch the fur?" Noah asks.

I bend and let him, removing his hand when it strays onto skin. I frequently worry that Noah will transition straight from trying to grab my boobs into exploring second base with his girlfriends, and hope he will give me a year or two of reprieve in between.

"Why are you all dressed up?" Anna, my nine-year-old,

asks as she enters the kitchen and joins the fray. The fray is why I *have* kids. I love the fray. And yet, sometimes I wish it would all vanish for just an hour so I could make Heath look at me. The way he used to look at me, like I was the only person in the room—or in the world.

"We're going to the Winter Festival, remember?"

"Tinsel and Tatas!" Noah cries, because somehow, even at the young age of seven, he is fully aware of every term for breasts.

That's the name of today's event: Tinsel and Tatas. All the proceeds from the games and gala will go to the Young Survival Coalition, an organization to educate, support, and inspire young breast cancer survivors. The whole family's going to the games, and then later, Heath and I will go to the gala.

An afternoon of fun, followed by a night of dancing, followed by Heath ripping my clothes off.

I flush a little, thinking about it, which tells you how dire the situation is. Or maybe just that the reindeer sweater is way too warm.

Anna frowns at me. "But isn't it all outside in the snow, Mom? Why are you wearing makeup? It's going to smudge."

When she is a little older, I know she will be my gal pal, but for right now, she is just another reminder that everyone in the world has an opinion about my outfit—except the man I wore it for.

"I wanted to be festive," I say, as cheerfully as I can manage.

"Should I be festive, too?" Anna wants to know. Lately, she is very concerned with doing things right, which is age appropriate for a newly minted tween. She's wearing a red-

and-green sweater festooned with fir trees and a pair of fleece pants.

"You're perfect." I clap my hands. "All right, Kennings! Go find your snow clothes, but don't put them on yet!"

As the kids scatter, I decide I'm going to give Heath one more try. After all, he looks absolutely delicious in a pair of not-at-all-dad jeans and a subtle maroon nod to Christmas sweaters that hugs his not-at-all-dad bod. One of Heath's strokes of brilliance when we had kids was to install a basement gym, and although I'm usually too exhausted to use it, he always seems to find time.

But before I can say something suggestive, or slink up to him and run my hands over his sweater-hugged pecs, he says, "Hey. If there's something special you want for Christmas, put it on your Amazon wish list."

Cue the sound of a Christmas carol record being scratched. Heath has never, ever asked me what he should get me for Christmas. Usually he's kind of a Christmas elf, and even when things have been chaotic, even the year that I was on bed rest with Kieran throughout the Christmas season, he's stepped up. So this feels like a new low.

I met Heath at college on a night when the snow was softly falling and the whole world was a winter wonderland. I still remember making snow angels with him, and the two of us watching a streetlight catch the individual flakes like silver stars, while my face, fingers, and toes froze because I didn't want to say goodnight.

We dated for ten blissful months, and then I found out I was pregnant.

Home from college on break, we were at my mom's for Christmas. I was terrified to tell Heath, but then I did, and he grabbed me and hugged me and said it was the best Christmas present ever. Three days later, on Christmas Eve, he danced me around the living room to "All I Want for Christmas Is You" and proposed. He'd even bought me a ring, while I was napping after a particularly brutal bout of nausea.

I used to think Christmas was the most romantic time of the year, but the last few years, it's been a slog. Buying gifts, buoying up the kids, and managing my own mostly unmet expectations.

I'm determined to turn that around, though.

All I want for Christmas, I think, is *us.*

CHAPTER 2
HEATH

Amanda leaves before me and the kids because her catering company, Around the Table, is working the games. She's gone about forty minutes before Noah scrapes his leg on the brick living room hearth.

I carry my wailing son to the bathroom and set him on the edge of the tub.

"Mommmmmmmmy! I want Mommy!"

You know what, bud? I think. *I want Mommy, too. Especially when she wears a scoop neck fur-lined sweater that clings to her curves and points the way to her gorgeous nipples. But we can't always have what we want.*

Obviously I don't say any of that out loud. There is so much I haven't said this year that I think I might be drowning in all of it.

I sigh.

"Mommy's not here, bud. She went to Tinsel and Tatas to get it ready for us so we can have a good time."

"Mommmmmmyyy!"

I rinse the cut with warm water. His wailing subsides—until I pull out the antibacterial lotion. Then he shrieks like I'm murdering him. Anna appears in the doorway. "What are you doing to him?" she accuses, pointing a small but mighty finger.

"I'm cleaning the cut so it won't get infected—"

Wrong move. Noah begins shrieking even louder, and Anna's eyes get huge. "Is that going to happen? Noah's gonna be infected?" she demands. I'd forgotten that she's very anxious these days about everything that can go wrong. Car crashes and heart attacks and, apparently, infected cuts.

"No, honey, it's not going to happen, because I'm cleaning it very carefully. He'll be just fine."

I succeed in disinfecting the cut (over Noah's screams), and his wailing subsides to hiccupy sobs.

Then I discover there are no band aids.

I could text Amanda and ask where they are, but I don't want to. I hate interrupting her at work.

I ransack every drawer and cabinet in the bathroom, every box that might have once held first aid items—but nothing.

"Anna, do you know where the band aids are?"

She shakes her head, vaguely pointing. "Mommy puts them there."

"Did they run out?"

"They might have," she says. Then, thoughtfully, "Noah and I did a crafts project with them."

I close my eyes.

"Sit here," I command Noah, and leave him, still wailing about how much it stings, while I go in search of anything I can use to cover the cut. The kitchen drawers are full of random trinkets, but no band aids. The pantry junk drawer is depleted of every last band aid except the small round ones for zits. Before I head out to ransack the first aid kit in my car, I zip upstairs again.

And end up in our bedroom, riffling through first my night table, then Amanda's, in the vain hope that I will find something—

My hand closes on a small, pink device, which immediately starts vibrating.

Whaaaatt?

I look behind me to make sure I have no witnesses and examine it. It looks a little like an ear thermometer, with a cone-shaped extension. But it's pink all over, and has a brand name on it. Hello Clitty. And there's a little logo, a disturbing picture of a cat face that looks more like—

The other kind of pussy.

My wife. Has a sex toy. In her night table. A sex toy that looks entirely capable of getting her off in a very, very sexy way.

My wife, who has not been interested in sex in...

I have been trying very, very hard—pun entirely intended—not to count—how long.

"Daaaaddddyyy!" Anna calls. "I found band aids!"

I set Hello Clitty back in the drawer, close it, and rejoin my children. I bandage Noah, walk both kids back downstairs. Kieran has scuttled ahead of us and I extract him from the pantry where he is sitting contently, finishing a box of Girl Scout thin mints. Then I say, because parenting is ninety-five percent improv, "If you liked band aid crafts, you'll love tape crafts," and set them up at the kitchen table with a roll of duct tape, a roll of electrical tape, a bunch of kiddie scissors, and a box of crayons.

Please God, don't let any of them figure out they can tie up the others.

While they're briefly but thoroughly engaged, I go into the other room, get out my computer and, disregarding the very real danger of permanently ruining my search history, google, "Hello Clitty."

And. Oh. Wow.

That thing? According to the reviews? It gives *really* good clit.

Has Amanda been...

I mean, presumably, Amanda *has* been.

When?

When I come to bed late?

When I get out of bed before her?

When she takes those long showers and spends a little extra time getting ready afterwards?

The visuals—the fantasy ones in my head—are pretty much killing me. My Amanda, flushed, lower lip slack, fingers parting her own folds, slowly bringing that little silicone cone to her eager clit...

Yeah.

I slam the laptop closed.

So. This changes everything.

Amanda and I are in a drought—we have been for way too long.

When I started my own business, I thought it would mean more freedom, but I was so wrong. Working for myself means that everything that goes wrong is my problem. I've finally gotten that under control, but only recently, finding programmers and project managers I can trust and stepping back from the day-to-day madness. So a lot of this drought is my fault.

But then Amanda started *her* business, and I was thrilled. I knew she was ready for something besides the kids, and I was sure she'd be happier once she could expend energy outside the house. And she is.

Except to be honest, that only makes it harder to keep my hands off her. She's full of good energy, chirpy and enthusiastic, and I absolutely love her when she's like that.

I mean, I love her all the time, but Amanda all fired up is sheer goddess material.

But by the time we get both kids in bed and fall in ourselves, totally exhausted...

I'm always, always hoping she'll turn to me, but it never happens anymore.

And I'm cautious because of what happened the last time I turned to her. She'd gotten woken up in the middle of the night because *two,* count 'em, *two* kids had peed their beds. We each changed a bed, then crawled back under the covers. She lay there, staring at the ceiling, looking wrecked, and I just wanted to—I don't know, give her some comfort. Some relief, some release. But when I reached for her, she turned to stone.

"Oh, fuck, Heath, *not you too,*" she said. "I feel like everyone wants a piece of me, a hundred percent of the time. Tell you what. If I want sex, I'll inform you, okay?" My heart shrank as she kept talking. "Otherwise, assume I don't."

Information received.

But now I have evidence that she *does* want... something. At least she wants orgasms.

And I want to be there when they happen.

I push the laptop away and head back into the kitchen.

"Kids," I say. "We're making a stop on the way to the games. Get dressed."

CHAPTER 3
AMANDA

Heath shows up with the kids while I'm helping Tessa, one of my employees, put the finishing touches on the hot drinks station. Of course the kids crowd around me in their snowsuits, demanding hot cocoa.

"Let's play first and drink cocoa after. To warm up," I tell them. I scrunch my fingers up in my gloves to warm them against my palms. It's the perfect day for this party, cold and crisp but brilliantly sunny. We're gathered at the base of a snow tubing hill at a local ski resort—another co-sponsor of the event.

"Noooooooo, cocoa!" Kieran wails.

Kieran was pretty easy-going as a two-year-old, but now he's fully embracing the terrible threes.

"Wouldn't you rather make a snow angel?" I ask him. There's a snow angel contest starting in fifteen minutes, and if we walk over now, we'll make it in time.

"Noooooooo, cocoa!" Kieran repeats.

"I've got this. You two go," a voice says from over my

shoulder. I turn to find Lucy, my brother Gabe's girlfriend, and Rachel, my brother Brody's girlfriend. They're bundled up in parkas, scarves, hats, and mittens, and yet both manage to be pink-cheeked and adorable, strands of Lucy's blond and Rachel's near-black hair escaping around their pretty faces. Since Lucy and Rachel came to town—and stayed—they've become two of my closest friends.

And, apparently, saviors.

"Where's Uncle Gabe?" Noah demands.

"He's running the snow tubing. Do you want to go tubing?" Lucy asks him.

"Yes!!!" Noah yells.

"Me too!" Kieran instantly forgets the cocoa. Unlike his older brother, he can't actually remember snow tubing, but he suspects that Uncle Gabe and Aunt Lucy will be more fun than his parents—and also that if Noah thinks something's a good time, it probably is.

Lucy smiles at me. "We've got the kids. You and Heath have some fun."

"You don't have to do that," Heath and I say, almost at the same time.

Lucy gives me a look. She knows things haven't been great between me and Heath for a while. Pretty sure Rachel does, too, because I might have had too much to drink at one of Rachel's sex-toy parties and admitted that my sex life isn't much of a party these days.

That was the same sex-toy party where I spent too much money on a personal pleasure device I have never used.

"Don't you want to spend time with Gabe and Brody?" I ask them.

"We'll have time later," Rachel says, with a shrug. I love both of them for not sharing too much about their super-amazing sex lives with my brothers (ewww), and for not being smug about how much sex they're having. Even though I'm the strongest advocate on earth for my brothers falling in love, getting married, and giving my kids cousins, I have to admit I'm jealous of Lucy and Rachel. I remember what it was like to be the center of someone's universe—the one he couldn't look away from.

The one he couldn't keep his hands off.

And maybe I'm bitter these days, too. Like, I've caught myself wanting to tell them, "You just wait! Diapers and Cheerios are the death of sex!"

But I'll never say it aloud. I'll never rain on anyone else's parade.

Heath is chasing after Kieran, who started for the snow tubing hill without an adult, and Anna and Noah are having a mini snowball fight off to the side, so I can whisper to Lucy and Rachel, "The sweater didn't work."

"The dress *will* work," Lucy says, with admirable certainty.

"What if it doesn't?" I ask. And, damn it, my voice cracks. Because the truth is, sometimes I worry that Heath feels trapped, that my getting pregnant with Anna meant he never got to choose this marriage.

Lucy and Rachel wrap me up in a hug.

"It's going to work," Rachel says. "And if it doesn't, there's always plan B."

Plan B is the lingerie I'm wearing under the dress.

We've done a lot of shopping recently.

"Let us do this for you," Lucy says, as Heath corrals

Kieran and Noah comes running up, crying because Anna put snow down his neck. I start to mediate, but Lucy squats and says, "Hey, Noah. Do you think you could show me how to ride a snow tube?"

And then the five of them are off, running towards the magic carpet, and Heath and I are left alone together, a little shellshocked, and suddenly, miraculously, kidless.

"Um, so... I was going to go make snow angels," I say to Heath.

His eyes meet mine, and I realize what a rarity that is lately. We don't look at each other much. Partly just because managing three kids doesn't leave time for gazing into each other's eyes. And partly because, well, it's surprisingly intense, and maybe we've forgotten how. I wait for him to look away, but he doesn't. There's something in his gaze I haven't seen for a long time. Curiosity. Interest. And maybe?

Heat.

Did I not see those things because they weren't there? Or purely because I hadn't looked?

Startled by the possibility that Heath isn't the only one not paying enough attention, I look away first.

"Snow angels sound really fun," he says. Then he surprises me by taking my mittened hand in his gloved one. Even through two layers of fabric, I can feel his warmth. My pulse kicks up. It's been a long time since Heath held my hand. I'd forgotten how good it feels.

We wander towards the snow angel field. It's set up in a

grid. Heath and I pick two squares next to each other, and I lie down, letting my legs fan out and flailing my arms. I lie there, staring up at the bright blue sky, feeling the cold soak into my limbs. It might be the most relaxed I've felt in... months. And I realize, this is what it's come to. Lying in the snow is the closest thing to a vacation I've had in way too long.

No wonder my marriage is a mess.

Then suddenly there is a ridiculously hot guy standing over me. Dark hair, dark eyebrows, beautiful medium-brown soulful eyes. Just a little bit of scruff on a strong jaw, and a full, lickable mouth. Something clenches in my low, low belly, accompanied by a spasm of guilt, because I'm married.

And then a second later, I realize, wait a second: That's Heath. That ridiculously hot guy? The one who still, after all these years, makes me melt?

That's my husband. A no-guilt proposition!

My heart pounds giddily. And then slows, because: I don't want to get my hopes up too high.

"Want me to help you up so you don't ruin the angel?" he asks quietly.

Just like the night we first met and made snow angels, Heath reaches down and grasps my hands. His are as strong as they were all those years ago, and he lifts me to my feet like I weigh nothing, bouncing me gently out of the snow, leaving a perfect angel behind.

Well, not perfect. My hat got left behind in the snow, red and pom-pommed and looking like it belongs to the angel.

We both laugh. He retrieves it and shakes off the snow.

He pushes my hair back from my face, sets the hat on my head and stands very close. I can see the flecks of caramel in his eyes. His breath, steaming from the cold, feathers across my cheeks.

I think he's going to kiss me, and my core tightens greedily, like in the oldest old days when he could get me going by staring at my mouth.

He's staring at my mouth now—

But instead of kissing me, he clears his throat and says, "So, Noah cut himself—not badly—" he interjects quickly, at the alarm on my face, "and I was looking for band aids."

"Shit." I remember, guiltily, that we're out, that it needed to go on the grocery list. I wonder if Heath wishes he had a wife who still had time to stay on top of the groceries and the cooking and the cleaning and the—

"Hey, where'd you go?" he asks.

"I was just thinking—I should have gotten band aids—"

He shakes his head. "That's not what I meant. Anyway, Anna found some. But I may have, um, ransacked your night table drawer, looking for them."

His eyebrows are way up, like he's trying to tell me something, but for the life of me I can't think what—

Oh, wait.

Yes, I can.

CHAPTER 4

HEATH

I haven't seen Amanda blush like that—because of something I did or said—in way too long. The pink flooding her cheeks is an injection of pure lust, straight to the bottom of my spine. Plus she's adorable with that stupid hat, and now I want to strip her out of her goddamned puffy coat so I can see her reindeer nose nipples and the fur neckline and all her curves.

She complains that she's gained weight with every pregnancy, and who knows, maybe it's factually true, but to me, she's perfect, just like always. To me, she only gets more beautiful the longer I know her.

I am about to reach a hand out, to cup the goofy hat and her snow-damp hair, to draw her towards me, but just then an announcement booms over the sound system—the snow tube races are starting. Amanda grabs my arm.

"What?"

"We have to race!"

Oh. Right. Amanda is madly competitive. If there's a

race, she has to enter it—and, preferably, win it. It may have something to do with having five brothers.

She may also be trying to avoid the conversation I started.

Whichever it is, instead of kissing her, I'm chasing her across the snow field to the magic carpet. But there are no doubles left, so we grab two singles and head up to the top. We're in two adjacent tracks. I look over at her and she looks at me and we're both smiling.

And suddenly I don't want to beat her at this race.

I want to win together.

At the very last minute, literally as the starting gun goes off, I jump out of my tube and behind Amanda, into her tube, and wrap my legs around her.

It's the kind of crazy thing we used to do all the time when we weren't trying to set a responsible example for three small kids, but beyond that, it's more physical contact than we've had in weeks. Months. We're hurtling downhill, wind in our hair and eyes and ears, and all I can focus on is the feel of her between my legs. Her soft body leans back against mine, and my own body is anything but soft right now. I lean forward and put my face against her hair, against her ear, and whisper, "You feel really good."

If she says anything in return, the wind catches it and whips it away, but her fingers dig deep into my thigh, and that's all the answer I need.

We win, probably because we weigh more combined than any other single tube. Amanda's brother, Gabe, who heads up Wilder Adventures, meets us at the bottom. "I have to ream you out publicly," he says in an undertone. "We're trying to recruit for our trips, and the last thing we need is for potential clients to think we let hotheads do stupid shit on our watch."

He proceeds to do exactly as promised: "Don't you *ever* do that again!" he roars.

"I'm sorry," I say, but I'm really not. I can still feel Amanda's hair against my cheek, her puffy-coat–clad breasts under my arms, her thighs between mine.

As Gabe completes his for-public-consumption lecture, I watch Amanda, the brightness in her eyes and that high flush on her face and throat. She's trying not to smile, which comes off as secret and mysterious in a way that makes me want to unwrap her from all those layers of winter clothes.

I feel a hard, sharp excitement, the kind you feel when you first meet someone. When you don't even know how it will feel to kiss them, or what sounds they'll make when you touch them.

Except this is Amanda, and I know. I know that when I whisper breath against the curve of her ear, she shivers and moans. And when I take a nipple in my mouth she huffs out air and grabs my head. When I slide down her body, she whimpers.

Snow pants are good armor against raging, inconvenient, snow party erections.

Gabe queues up the next race, and Amanda tugs my arm, dragging me over to the side of the hill.

"So," she says. "You searched my night table."

I nod.

"And you found Hello Clitty."

I admit that I did. "Why do you need that thing?"

I mean to ask it neutrally, but I sound exactly like a

jealous husband. Like I caught her kissing another guy in a closet somewhere, and I'm ready to do violence.

She raises an eyebrow. "For clitoral stimulation," she says.

"Yes," I say. "I got that. But you have me. For clitoral stimulation."

"Do I?" she asks.

"You know you fucking do," I growl.

CHAPTER 5

AMANDA

Heath. Is. Jealous.

Of a vibrator.

If things were even slightly different between us, that would make me laugh.

But this is...

This is good.

"So let me get this straight," I say. "You're jealous of a vibrator."

"That thing is *not* just a vibrator." His eyes are hot on mine. "It's like the famed Swedish electro-suck machine! You brought serious competition into the house!"

He's half joking, but definitely no more than half. His jaw's tight with real frustration.

Yeah, Heath, me too. Frustration has been my middle name for way too long.

"I didn't think—"

I feel like once the words are out of my mouth, everything will change. And even though that's what I want, it's kind of terrifying too. As much as I hate how things are now, I *know* how they are. If we get honest about where we are, what if...

What if, in the end, honesty drives us apart instead of bringing us back together? What if Heath does feel trapped, like he never made a choice, and if being frank with each other gives him an out?

I take a deep breath, and feel the answer in my soul: If that's what happens, then that's what happens, but we can't keep going like we have been.

"I didn't think you cared about our sex life," I confess, tears prickling my eyes.

I've startled him—and then his expression softens, his eyes warm. "Oh, Jesus, Amanda. You have no idea, do you? I lie in that bed next to you, and all I can think about is what I want to do to you."

The words suck the breath right out of my lungs.

"You—you do?"

He nods. His eyes are so full of heat, I can feel it flash up in my core.

"So why don't you ever... do... those...things?"

"You told me not to."

Another race finishes on the hill, a wave of tubers yelling and congratulating each other, but I can't look at anything except him. "I—what?!"

"You remember that night, when Noah and Kieran both wet the bed, and then I tried to kiss you." He hesitates. "And you said—" Lowers his voice. "'Everyone wants a piece of me and if I want sex, I'll inform you. Otherwise, assume I don't.'"

"I never said that!"

But things are starting to make a little more sense. How things went from bad to, well, non-existent in our intimate life.

"You did," he says, not a shadow of doubt in his warm-as-hot-buttered-rum voice.

"Oh, God, Heath, are you sure? I literally have no memory of saying that. Are you sure I was conscious when I said it?"

"I mean, you said the words out loud. They made perfect sense, even if I didn't want to hear them. You sounded awake."

I cover my face with mittened hands, burying my cheeks in wet, icy wool. I can't look at him. And then I do and manage to say, "God, I've been wondering why it's like the English channel between us in that god-forsaken bed."

"Are you telling me...?" he growls. "Are you saying...?"

I drop my hands. "I'm saying, Heath, don't assume I don't want sex! Assume I do! And if I don't, I'll tell you. And I have no idea what weird form of sleep deprivation or temporary insanity I was operating under that night, but for fuck's sake: Do. Not. Believe. Anything. I. Say. In. The. Middle. Of. The. Night."

He grabs me and places one wet mitten on each of my cheeks. Lowers his face to mine. And kisses me. Not gently and lovingly. Not family friendly. Nope. He's all possession and need. A hard, hot sweep of tongue, both his hands on my head, a groan into my mouth.

And I love it.

He breaks the kiss and we both look around guiltily, but luck is on our side and no one seems to be paying attention. Because a new race is starting.

"I need you alone," he says simply, and I can feel the words like the stroke of fingers between my legs.

I pull my phone out and text Lucy. *Taking a quick walk in the woods.*

 *Glad to hear it.*

IT'S NOT hard to find a quiet corner at a big ski resort. Just a short distance off one of the many groomed paths, there's a snowshoe track that someone must have made earlier this morning. He tugs me along it until we can't see or hear the Games anymore, and steers me so my back is against a big tree. And then he kisses me again, just like before. It's not a kiss you give to warm up someone you're unsure of. It's the way you kiss someone who's a sure thing, someone you plan to be fucking in just a few minutes.

And it's so unbelievably hot.

His mouth is open over mine, his tongue bossy and sure, his mittens hitting the snow, his bare hands unzipping my jacket and finding my reindeer noses.

"This sweater," he growls.

"I thought you didn't notice."

"I notice everything you do, Amanda."

My mittens hit the snow just like his, and I sink my fingers into the softness of his hair.

He noses along the fur edge, mouth hot on my skin. I want him to push the neck of my sweater down and bury his face in my breasts, but I also don't want to freeze to death. I pull his head back up for more of those kisses, because my mouth is the hungriest part of me. I feel like I've been waiting for this for so long, like a starving woman at the Heath buffet. And he totally obliges, licking into me, sucking my lower lip, biting hard enough to make me yelp, then soothing the spot with his tongue. We devour each other, and not just with our mouths. His hands are under the reindeer now, fingers homed in on where my breasts are tight and aching, pulled to brutal peaks that need him so badly. When he touches my nipples, I whimper and rock my hips.

Even with two puffy coats and two pairs of snow pants between us, I can feel Heath's erection, hard, hot, and oh, so welcome. And bonus: the way two layers of nylon slide against each other? Who knew?

It's a whole new marketing opportunity for the snow pants company people.

Heath has caught my rhythm, and he's stroking himself against my sex, slow, steady, and just the way I need it. The suggestion of friction is maddening, the muffled pressure perfect for the building tension between my legs, tugged ten times tighter by the skilled flick of his thumbs on my nipples.

It's been so, so long. The orgasm is right there, so easy. I don't even have to reach for it. Heath does it all.

"I'm going to—"

And then I'm coming, strong, sweet waves of pleasure, the muscles clenching in my core and lower belly, Heath's mouth covering mine to drown the sounds I'm making.

"Jesus, Amanda," he says, his cheek against mine, his breath hot in my ear. "No one has ever been that sexy before with that many clothes on."

And—most miraculously of all—we are laughing together.

I think if it had been just me, I would have left it like that.

But Heath is definitely a better person than I am.

"We should talk," he says.

CHAPTER 6
HEATH

She gives me an incredulous look.

"You want to... talk? With this going on...?" She slides her palm under my parka, into the waistband of my snow pants, under the waistband of my base layer. "Damn," she says. "Commando."

She is smiling and pink-cheeked and so, so beautiful.

"It's not commando if you're wearing long underwear."

"It is in my book." She wraps her fist, which is miraculously, somehow, warm, around my erection. "We could talk in a few minutes," she whispers.

Any guy who makes it out of high school alive knows that there are hand jobs—and then there are hand jobs. Amanda wasn't born Goddess of the Hand Job, but from the beginning, she paid attention. She listened, she asked me to show her, and she figured it out. Firm grip, pressure on the underside, a thumb teasing the head with each pass.

She figured out how to do it better than I can, and holy *fuck* have I missed her.

"A few minutes would be okay," I grind out, as her palm twists exactly right around my primed-to-burst cock.

She tilts her face up, asking for another kiss, and I've missed that, too, the taste of her. This kiss is so familiar but also so new: her lips cold, her mouth hot. She's working my cock and the fabric between my legs slides over my balls, and—"Amanda!" My orgasm boils up from down deep, raging and all-consuming—long, thick spasms of pleasure and release.

She swallows my cries and draws the last of the orgasm out of me so expertly that I'm wrung out. When she licks her palm, cleaning herself up, my body clenches again as if she's tongued me.

Then she folds herself into my arms and sighs contentedly, and that might be the part I like best.

We stand like that a long time, our hands tucked into each other's clothing for warmth.

"I've missed you," she says.

"I've missed you, too."

"Let's not do that again."

I shake my head. But we both also know it's not that easy. "It's been really hard recently."

Her turn to nod. "We're both doing so much and we never catch up. Sometimes I get so mad, knowing you're in the gym working out, and I'm trying desperately to get on top of the yard work."

"I know," I tell her. "I feel that way when you're watching Netflix and I'm trying to get the kitchen into a state that even vaguely resembles clean. I know you're doing everything you can and you need a break too, but it just feels so unfair."

"And then I get into bed and I'm just dead," she says. "And sometimes I think about it, about reaching for you, but all I'm capable of doing is sleeping."

"We need to figure out how to get more help."

She nods.

"Maybe pay some people to do stuff—clean the house, do the yardwork—now that both businesses are going great guns."

"I don't ever want to go back to where we were before today," I say. Because I want to keep her smiling and pink like this.

"Me neither," she agrees, fervently.

I can't help my non-stop smile. "Can we make a deal? More sex, less housework?"

She grins. "That sounds like a deal I can absolutely get behind."

"And more childcare, too?"

"Yeah. Absolutely."

"And I need to assume you want sex from now on."

The corners of her mouth tug up. "A new default setting."

"Or just factory reset. Because I used to assume you always wanted sex."

That makes her laugh, the idea of factory reset.

Amanda's sexual eagerness is one of the things I've always loved about her. She and I were both always good-to-go in college—and even up through when Noah was born. It just got more and more complicated after that—multiple kids, my business being so in need of my attention, and then Kieran and then her business...

It was a slow slide, and somehow we didn't notice.

She sinks back into my hug, quiet for a moment. I bend my head to inhale the vanilla-and-snowy-day scent of her hair. I would like to stay like this for hours, holding her in my arms in the woods, but my toes are starting to freeze and we've left Lucy with our three hooligans, and I know we can't hang out in the quiet, snow-decked woods forever.

I would if I could, if I knew we could be like this all the time.

CHAPTER 7
AMANDA

As we walk back to find the kids, I'm *happy*.

A bit damper than I started out, but in a very good way. Boneless from that orgasm, which was one of the best I've ever had and will go in the bubble bath film archive. But I'm also just contented in a way I can't remember being in... years. And maybe it's just sex hormones, but maybe it's not.

I feel like I got something back I'd lost, something precious.

I'm also horny, because apparently you can't make up for an epic drought with one orgasm. But even that makes me feel hopeful. We'll go to the gala tonight and then afterwards...

Mmm.

My core clenches pleasantly, aftershocks and anticipation co-mingled. It's actually almost... vibrating?

Nope, that's my phone. I pull it out and answer before I can fully register who's calling.

"Mrs. Kenning?"

Almost no one calls me Mrs. Kenning. Only—

Oh, *shit*.

"I'm so, so sorry," the babysitter, Lulu, says. "I just threw up five times and—"

The only thing worse than missing the gala tonight would be three kids with stomach flu, so I say, quickly, "No. Please don't give it another thought," even as a weight settles in my gut. "Take care of yourself, rest up, and I hope you feel better super quickly."

I end the call and turn to Heath, but he already knows. His jaw, which had reached a point of near total slackness shortly after he came all over my hand, is tight again. He looks like stressed-out work Heath, the Heath I don't ask for help because I know he'll give it, but only at the expense of his own sanity.

"Canceled?" Frustration vibrates in his voice. "God. After you deliberately turned down catering the gala so we could both go. And all the family babysitters are going, of course."

Everyone in the Wilder family will be at the gala except my middle brother, Clark. He's been keeping to himself a lot since his wife's death eighteen months ago, and parties aren't his thing. We try not to ask a lot of him these days, so he's not a candidate for babysitting three kids.

The best bets would be Lucy, Rachel, or my mom, but no way either of us wants to deprive Lucy or Rachel of the chance to experience the gala, and my mom, as a survivor, will be speaking tonight.

I pocket my phone and we continue our walk back to the snow tubing hill, picking up the main cat track. The hill comes into view ahead of us, dotted with tubers, and I hear their shouts of excitement.

"Could Hanna babysit?" Heath asks. Hanna is the fourth woman in my growing friend group, and my brother Kane's business partner at Wilder. She's an honorary Wilder, even though she has her own set of five rowdy brothers.

I shake my head. "No. She's actually kind of excited to go to the gala. We had to drag her kicking and screaming to buy gala clothes, but then a couple nights ago, she grudgingly admitted that she was actually looking forward to getting dressed up, as long as we knew she wasn't wearing makeup or getting her hair done."

Hanna can usually be counted on to boycott anything that falls remotely in the "girly" realm, but not this time.

Heath gets it: You don't pass up an opportunity to see Hanna in a dress. His shoulders are set. "I'll stay home with them."

"No," I say firmly. "You haven't gotten out or gone anywhere in months. I've at least had a few girls nights here and there. You go."

He shakes his head. "But you'll enjoy it more. It's more your thing than mine. And you bought a dress."

"You rented a tux."

He frowns. "Amanda, I can't help you if you won't let me."

"I don't want you to help me if it's going to make you miserable. I hate it when you're miserable. The way you sit there and I can see in your shoulders and your jaw you're unhappy, but you don't say anything. It's like we're having a contest to see who can suffer in silence more manfully..."

"It's not a contest, Amanda." His voice is tight and hard. It feels like we're moving back an hour to before we got each other off against a tree. "Not everything I feel or do is about you..."

"But..." My voice verges on shouting. "I never said it was! You just think if you show any weakness or admit anything is hard, the world is going to end! I know you feel trapped. I know you didn't choose this—"

He turns, his face as hard as his voice was a moment ago, and I know he's going to say something I don't want to hear.

But just then, Anna comes running up.

"Mommy! Daddy! Come quick! There's a snowball fight, and we need you!"

CHAPTER 8

HEATH

I know you feel trapped. I know you didn't choose this.

Does she really think that?

God. I need her to understand how wrong she is, but she has already taken off with Anna, back toward the snow angel field.

I race to catch up, then reach for her arm. "Amanda."

"Heath, you're on blue—Amanda, you're on red—"

Her brothers are issuing instructions, and the moment is lost in a whirl of assembling snowball teams. And maybe it's for the best. I don't know what Amanda will say, and I don't want us to fight in front of Anna.

My team, which includes both Anna and Kieran, hunches down behind a snow wall, prepping piles and piles of snowballs and hashing out strategy like we're the only hope to save the galaxy. The adults are going to launch a straightforward offensive plus take the brunt of the defense, while the kids sneak around the flanks and throw snowballs behind their walls.

I come out roaring, flinging snowballs and war cries. At first we're driven back by the force of their assault, but they use up their pre-made ammo quicker than we do, and we regain lost ground. Better still, we succeed in distracting them from the offensive the kids are launching, and I can hear my kiddos, among others, whooping as they come in from behind.

As anyone who's ever had a snowball fight knows, you can't be serious when you're having one. It's like as the snowballs break apart, so does anything you're holding inside—anger, frustration, fear. They melt away—at about the same time snow is starting to melt down your neck. And three-year-old Kieran strikes only cuteness into our hearts.

Still, I'm committed to the win, so I chase an opposing player, hurling hastily packed snowballs. Then I realize it's Amanda. And she's a worthy opponent, throwing snowballs with deadly aim, showing off her high school softball skills. I was never a baseball player, and my football spiral doesn't seem to be translating to snow. What choice do I have? I run her down and drop a whole load of snow on her head. Whereupon she grabs handfuls to shove in my face, and we end up falling in the snow, wrestling, laughing. She's squirming under me, her soft thighs cradling me, as I tickle her.

Then we're kissing, mouths steaming, hands groping, like we're alone.

"Aaaaah!" Amanda says, when my hands find a patch of warm bare skin at her waist. "Not the mittens!"

Which reminds us it's a family show, and we quit, sitting in the snow, wet, cold, and—

Still laughing.

She stops laughing first.

"Heath." Her voice is somber. So much so that I'm momentarily afraid again.

But I gather my courage and speak. "What you said. About me feeling trapped. You're wrong about that. I always wanted this. Anna was a surprise, but a good one. I wanted you in my life forever. I've never felt trapped. Never. If I had to do it over again, I would choose it again in a heartbeat."

Her eyes get huge, then fill with tears.

"Did you really doubt that?"

I yank off my mittens and wipe away her tears, one by one, and she doesn't even complain about my ice-cold fingers.

"Please don't doubt it. Please promise me you won't. Ever again."

I pull her into my arms, and hold her as tight as I can. She holds me right back.

When she finally lets go, she says, "I think either we should both go to the gala or neither of us should go."

We sit on that for a moment.

"If neither of us goes?"

"We could Netflix and chill," she says, with a naughty smile that almost—but not quite—makes me pick option A. The thing that sways me is that there is nothing I love more than Amanda in a fancy dress. I try really hard to be a sensitive twenty-first century guy, but I love my wife all fancy, in high heels, and clutching my arm for balance. Dancing with me and only me.

It's been so fucking long.

I want that tonight.

And I know she does, too.

We hold eye contact for a long moment. Not sexual this time, but: *We can do this. Together.*

I take a deep breath and ask, "Do you think the other thing you said is true? About me not showing weakness?"

She closes her eyes, then opens them, and her expression's different. Soft.

"I think it's true of both of us, Heath. Neither of us is good at showing weakness. Or asking for help, which is sort of the same thing."

I think about the moment when I couldn't find the band aids. I could have texted Amanda, but I didn't. Because I didn't want to interrupt her.

And maybe because I didn't want to be the guy who couldn't just handle it on my own. I mean, band aids?

"No," I agree. "Neither of us is good at asking for help."

I shed my mitten and cup her face. Lean in, and kiss her cold mouth, seeking the heat inside her. I want to bury myself in that heat. And I will, later. After I dance with her all night and make her want it so much she's whimpering.

"Let's not just *say* we need to ask for help. Let's do it." I pull out my phone.

"Who are you texting?" she asks.

"The whole family list," I tell her. Which at this point includes brothers, girlfriends, and an assortment of family friends.

And right away, my phone starts buzzing. I hold it up so she can see. There's a string of answers. Suggestions, ideas, friends of friends.

"Guess we're both going to the gala," I say, and she leans close, resting her cheek against mine, and it's better than anything.

CHAPTER 9
AMANDA

"You ready?" I've just completed a final check of myself in our bedroom mirror.

"Can't wait." Heath's standing at the bottom of the stairs, waiting for me to descend in my gala finery. I step slowly, aware that this is an echo of our wedding, when I braved the stairs of the Five Rivers Lodge on Gabe's arm, Heath gazing up at me worshipfully.

Gabe's not here, of course, but the anticipation feels very much the same, the breath caught in my chest, the hum of excitement in my belly, and lower.

Heath's gaze sweeps down my body, pausing to take in the dress. It's Christmas-green velvet, with an empire waist and a super-flattering sweetheart neckline. His eyes, when they meet mine again, are gratifyingly dark. So intense and aware that the knot in my core tightens.

He opens his mouth, but nothing comes out. Struck speechless is pretty awesome.

I was trying for serious and wistful, but I can't help it—I grin.

"Wow." He's recovered his powers of speech. "Wow, wow, wow, Amanda. You are so fucking beautiful."

That's pretty good, too.

"You're not so bad yourself, handsome," I tell him, and he grins, too, white teeth in a face that's perfectly tanned from a day outdoors. My heart skips a couple of beats. There has definitely not been enough of Heath grinning in my life lately.

Heath looks...

Heath looks like sex on a stick.

This man cleans up *nice*.

He's wearing a rental tux that fits like it was made for him, and he fills it out like a man who has a very expensive gym in his basement. (Best decision I ever co-made.) The crisp white shirt and rich deep black contrast impeccably, and make his eyes look even warmer and his soft mouth redder and more kissable.

I step forward to test out whether it feels as good as it looks, and, *yup*.

I'm very much looking forward to returning here with my husband after the gala.

Meanwhile, during the gala, our kids will stay with Rachel's parents, who had already been recruited to watch Brody's son, Justin. I quizzed them extensively about adding three more to the fray, but they said the three older kids would keep baby Justin entertained and make their jobs easier. So it's animated movie and sleepover night at the Perezes.

Which means Heath and I are alone in the house for the first time in... years? Heath, who has... just dropped to his knees?

"Sweetie—?" I tug on his shoulders. "You're going to ruin your pants."

"Don't care." His voice is muffled by green velvet as he eases my heavy skirt up, sorts out the crinoline and liner, and finds my bare thigh with his mouth.

"Oh, Jesus, Amanda. These fucking panties." He licks my thigh and runs a finger along my seam, through the lace.

"A little higher," I instruct greedily, not caring whether we ruin my dress or make it to the gala at all. But he doesn't obey. Instead, he tugs my panties down and whips something out of his pocket.

Hello Clitty.

I'm going to have recurrent dreams about this, my tux-wearing husband with a sex toy in his hands, under my skirts.

"I'm doing an A/B test," he informs me. He switches it on and brings the little buzzing silicone cone to my clit.

And it feels good. Really good. Especially when he situates it just right, so it tugs on the hood of my clit, and his fingers work their way into me, slick with my need for him.

The gentle suction is perfect, but…

It's a little…

Dunno. Sterile?

Still, when he takes it away, I whimper. "Heath," I complain.

He sticks his head out from under my skirt, smirking.

"That was part one of the test," he says. "This is part two."

Then he opens his mouth over my pussy.

Oh. Yeah. Wow.

Heath is—

Heath is the king of head. He has this thing he does—

He's doing it now. Sucking, super gently, and then, sometimes, mixing it up by flicking me with his tongue. He can wind me up in seconds flat.

Everything in me is tight. Nipples, the muscles in my belly, my inner thighs. I'm poised right on the edge for him.

And then he stops. And stands up.

"Heath," I protested. "You can't—"

"I want you to be thinking about it all night," he says. "I want you to be eating your dinner and thinking about my tongue. I want you to be dancing with me and thinking about my cock."

"I'm not going to be able to think about anything else."

"Good."

"Part two," I say. "Part two wins."

He grins and licks his lips. "I know, baby. There was never any doubt about that."

The Tinsel and Tatas Gala is in full swing.

Someone with brilliant decorating skills has thoroughly decked the halls of the Depot Hotel so the Western-themed decor fades into the background and Christmas glitter shines forth.

Long evergreen swags hang in red-ribboned loops, and fairy lights glimmer everywhere. The tables are decorated with candles in gold-and-glass holders, red napkins, and more swags.

The band has been playing Christmas favorites for hours, and right now most of the Wilders are on the dance floor, getting down to Brenda Lee's "Rockin' Around the Christmas Tree." Heath and I are giddy with joy, surrounded by our favorite people.

You would never peg Lucy for a hard-partier, but that girl can *dance* when she lets her hair down, and after a few glasses of Christmas punch, she is going to town opposite Gabe, the two of them grinning at each other like Christmas fools. Strands of her blond hair frizz around her face, and I watch as my ordinarily uber-serious oldest brother tucks a strand behind Lucy's ear and plants a kiss on her nose.

Meanwhile Brody and Rachel are more restrained, but still pretty dang cute, my scowly bad-boy brother all soft-eyed and totally besotted with Rachel, who somehow manages to look a lot like a sexy librarian (perfect for her dual careers), with her hair knotted up, wearing a nip-waist blouse and black flowy pants.

And the thing is? I realize I'm not jealous of either of them. Or remotely bitter. Now I want to say to them: You know how you feel right now, tonight? Remember that, because it's what you need to recapture when times get tough.

And make sure you ask for help.

That's what I'd tell them.

Remember why you love each other, and ask for help.

I'm feeling the Christmas spirit for the first time in years. I'm so excited to be here with my extended family, celebrating for a good cause, knowing I have the hottest husband in the world. (Aaand he's a great dad who does housework.)

Also, in an A/B test against the top rated sex toy in Rachel's company's arsenal, he comes out ahead.

Pun intended.

"You're joking, right?"

Hanna—in the most basic little black dress on earth—and my brother Easton have just come into view, and that's Hanna's outraged voice.

"No, I'm not going to dance with you. Aren't there enough other innocent victims here? Or have you slept with and alienated the entire population of Rush Creek?"

Ah. Some things never change. Hanna and Easton will always be oil and water.

The song ends and Heath and I head back to the table to slake our thirst (for beverages, people, for beverages). For the first time, I notice the gorgeously lit Christmas tree behind Heath's seat.

It's decorated entirely with crocheted tata ornaments.

Heath's gaze follows mine. "Noah would love that."

I give him side-eye. I wasn't aware Heath understood the extent of our son's tata obsession, but I should have known. He doesn't miss much. "And I'm glad he'll never see it. We'd never be able to tear him away."

"Excellent point." He grins. We sit down and drink half a pitcher of water between us before we're restored to our normal selves. The punch is strong, on top of everything else.

Heath's jacket is hung over the back of his chair. His hair is a mess. His bowtie is draped around his neck. Two buttons of his shirt are open, revealing his strong tanned chest and a little bit of dark hair.

He looks like a guy who just got his mind blown in some secret corner of the party.

Which gives me an idea I might put into use later...

But before I can suggest anything, Heath says, "Hey."

His expression is super serious.

"I want to give you your Christmas gift early. While we're here together. I have a few other things for you, but this one is special."

"What happened to my Amazon wish list?"

He shakes his head. "That—that was a moment of weakness. I promise, it'll never happen again."

Something about the earnest expression on his face tells me he means it.

He reaches into his pocket and pulls out a small box.

And it's crazy because I've been married to him almost ten years, but my heart pounds like it did when he took out a similar box and opened it to show me my engagement ring.

He opens this one, and nestled in the black velvet is an unfamiliar but beautiful sapphire and diamond eternity wrap that will fit perfectly around my engagement ring opposite my wedding band.

"Wait—when did you—?"

"On the way here. The kids helped me pick it out. I realized it was way past time to tell you that in a heartbeat, I'd marry you again, Amanda."

"Heath—" I'm breathless as he slides the ring on my finger. It looks just right.

"I love you, Amanda."

"I love you, too, Heath."

And right then, of course, "All I Want for Christmas Is You" comes on. For all today's ups and downs, all the big emotions, releases and relief, that's the thing that almost wrecks me.

And Heath, being Heath, can see it in my eyes. He strokes one finger across my cheek, catching a single tear as it falls.

"Time to go home?" he asks, uncertainly. Gently.

I shake my head and smile at him, this beautiful man, my beloved husband. "No," I say. "Time to dance."

And we dance and dance.

They finally have to shoo us off the dance floor and send us home to our quiet, temporarily kid-less house.

For one night, we've got an empty house.

And we *know* how to use it.

Thank you so much for reading *Wilder for the Win!* Love Amanda? Then you'll want to read *Make Me Wilder*, the book that introduces her. It's the story of how city girl Lucy sheds her high heels to help the mountain men of Wilder Adventures retool their outdoorsy business for the spa-and-wedding crowd. And how much business owner Gabe Wilder hates the idea...grab *Make Me Wilder* now!

Go to geni.us/MakeMeWilder

Keep reading for an excerpt from *Make Me Wilder*!

EXCERPT FROM MAKE ME WILDER
LUCY

I almost choke on my coffee. Liam is here—with flowers.

I can see him through the conference room window. He strides toward me, a big bouquet in his hands, every bit as hot as that night, six weeks ago, when I hooked up with him after the comedy show.

I never thought I'd see him again. We'd agreed it was just a one-night thing, and at the time, I was totally okay with that.

But in the weeks since then, I've been regretting not getting his number, or giving him mine. He was fun to talk to and good in bed, traits that are rare by themselves and a unicorn together. I've thought about trying to look him up, track him down. How many Liam Johnsons could there be in Manhattan?

Um, yeah. Quite a few. So I didn't even go there. We'd agreed. And I didn't want to be a stalker.

But now that he's here, I'm remembering how hot he is: slightly ginger-y blond hair, dazzling blue-green eyes, and a killer hard-won gym bod. All packaged today in a gray suit, black button-down, and silver-and-blue tie.

And he brought me flowers.

He opens the conference room door, and I rise out of my seat, ready to run to him. In my whole life, no guy has ever shown up at my work with flowers. This is a grand gesture. He found me, he came to my workplace with flowers, and now he's walked into the middle of a brainstorming session with my boss, Gennie, and two of my other female coworkers.

I think I just fell in love with Liam at second sight.

If this were a movie, I'd run into his arms and kiss him, but I hold back, because this isn't the movies, and my boss is here.

"Oh my God, Liam," I say. "How did you find me?"

Gennie turns to look at me.

Both of my coworkers turn to look at me.

Liam turns to look at me.

Wait a second.

Why wasn't Liam looking at me?

I realize that Gennie has stood up. And taken two steps toward Liam. Confusion is written all over her face.

My coworkers don't look confused. They look horrified.

I am very slowly—like slow-motion car wreck slowly—piecing this together.

Liam is not here with flowers for me.

He is here with flowers for my boss.

And I said that thing aloud. The thing about *how did you find me?* We all heard it. Liam. Gennie. Jasmine and Pilar.

"It's not what it looks like," Liam says. To Gennie. "Gennie, whatever you think, it's not that."

"If you'll excuse me," Gennie says. She doesn't say what she will do. She just picks up her laptop and her iPad and her notebook, stacks them neatly. Gennie is always calm, always deliberate. She is calm and deliberate now as she takes her things and walks out of the conference room, Liam hurrying after her with the flowers, turning to give me a look that is both apologetic and chiding.

"Um," Jasmine says. "I should—"

She and Pilar get up. Both move toward the door.

"Wait!" I call.

They reluctantly turn back.

"Help?"

They exchange a look. In their faces I see all the questions that any sane woman would have in this situation. Should their loyalty to Gennie trump everything? If they stay, will they be betraying her?

And if they go, won't they miss out on the chance to find out what the hell is going on?

"I have to get back to work," Jasmine says. Not a surprising decision. Jasmine is Gennie's best work friend. She slips out of the conference room without a backward glance.

But Pilar hangs back. She gives me a sympathetic look.

"What did you do?" she whispers.

"I didn't know he was her boyfriend," I whisper back. Oh, *God*. I'm dead. I'm fired. I'm dead and fired and jobless and did I mention dead?

Also, I'm a terrible person who sleeps with other

women's boyfriends. But I'm not that person. I swear I'm not. I would never knowingly be that person.

Could I accidentally be that person? Apparently.

"I didn't know." My voice is a tiny, wispy thread.

"She can't fire you if you didn't know," Pilar says.

I never said *fired* out loud, but apparently that is where both our minds have gone, which isn't reassuring at all.

This is a terrible time to be flooded with passionate love for my job, but that's what's happening. I love, love, love my job. I love marketing and I love working for a really good marketing company and I love figuring out how to market goods and services to women, which is what our team specializes in. Gennie is a generous boss, fair and creative. Jasmine and Pilar are excellent colleagues. Besides, to survive in New York City, I need an income.

"How long have they been a couple?" I madly hope she will say less than six weeks.

"Two years."

I shrink like a poked slug.

"But they broke up three months ago and only just got back together." Pilar holds up hopeful crossed fingers.

Salvation.

"It was six weeks ago."

Pilar nods. "That was when they were broken up." Her eyebrows draw together. "But how did you not recognize him?"

"I've never met him."

"Didn't you meet him at the Christmas party?"

"I wasn't at the Christmas party." My voice is small again.

"You weren't at the Christmas party?"

The Grand Plan Christmas party is not to be missed. But I did. I shake my head. "I had—other plans."

I told myself that this year, at this job, I would finally do things differently. I wouldn't hang back like a shy preschooler sussing out the playground vibe. I wouldn't say *no* when I should say yes, then make lame excuses. I'd go to the effing Christmas party.

After the e-vite went out with the details, I kept meaning to buck up, put on my big girl pants, and show the hell up... but while I was waiting for the injection of courage that never came, I missed the RSVP deadline.

So I stayed home, ate Ben & Jerry's and watched *Die Hard* and *Love Actually*.

But I don't tell her any of that.

"Well, what about Friday night happy hour? I know he's stopped by a few times—" I can almost hear the "tick, tick, tick" of Pilar's brain working through this puzzle and arriving at a conclusion. "But you've never come out to happy hour, have you?"

"No," I say.

"And you don't follow any of us on social media."

Now she sounds like she's adding up my crimes. Calculating out my sentence.

I shake my head.

"Why not?"

"I only use social media for work," I say.

"But happy hour?" The way she says 'happy hour' makes me feel so nerdy.

"I—" I gulp air. "I should go pack my desk."

I sneak one last glance at Pilar, who looks at me with so much pity that I have to quickly turn away.

I've just finished packing my desk when Gennie calls me to her office. Seated behind her big, bossy desk, she has never looked so cold and intimidating, not even on the day I interviewed with her, a year and a half ago. And that was one of the scariest interviews I've ever done, though later I realized that Gennie reserves that side of her personality for interviewees. And as I discover today, for employees who sleep with her boyfriend.

"I am so, so, so sorry, Gennie. You have to believe me, I had no idea who he was."

"I do believe you," she says, her voice as terrifying as her demeanor.

"I would never. Never in a million years. Girl code..."

I apparently can no longer complete sentences. My eyes fill with tears, but I *won't cry*. I won't.

There's something in people that senses weakness, my mother said, after we left Atwell, the small town that soured me on small towns. *They sense it and they go in for the kill.*

Gennie looks like she would like to kill me.

"Do you even understand why I'm so angry?" she says.

"You have every right to be mad! I slept with your boyfriend! Not that I knew he was your boyfriend. And not when he was your boyfriend. But the fact remains, I did. If I were in your shoes, I'd be furious with me."

I suddenly realize it doesn't matter whether or not she is going to fire me. I have to do the right thing. I've made things impossible. Uncomfortable. And whether I did it on purpose or not, it's my fault. There's only one way out. I'll have to quit.

"I want to make this as easy for you as possible," I say quietly. "I'll give you my letter with two weeks notice as soon as we're done in here."

Gennie's perfect eyebrows nearly touch her hair. "Lucy." I brace myself. "I'm not mad because you accidentally slept with my boyfriend when he wasn't actually my boyfriend. I mean I am. Of course I am. I want to strangle you with my bare hands and bury the body where it can never be found. Mmmm. Actually, I want to strangle him with my bare hands and bury the body where it can never be found. Or?" She tilts her head. "Strangle both of you?"

I wince.

"Sorry. Too much honesty? It's just, he wasn't supposed to rebound. He was supposed to pine and realize how much he'd taken me for granted." She sighs. "Which he did, eventually, but he may have slept with half of Manhattan on his way to doing it."

Gennie comes out from behind the desk, pacing. She kicks off her heels and strides back and forth in her stockinged feet. Then she stops, turns, and points at me. "But whatever, I get it, you didn't know, and he didn't know who you were. He was just, you know, doing what guys do when they're hurt." She crosses her arms. "But I'm mad at you because if you had even *once* come out to happy hour with us, or gone to a Christmas party or a rooftop barbecue or a housewarming party for anyone at work, or followed even one of us on Facebook or Instagram or... you would have known who Liam was." Her voice has gained strength and her finger is jabbing the air. I take a step back.

"I'm mad at you because I've been working with you for more than a year and you literally have no idea what's going on in my life, none! And I literally have no idea what's going on in yours. I didn't know you like comedy clubs or sometimes hook up with strangers—"

I wince, but there's no judgment in Gennie's voice. Just... sadness.

"And if you'd just let any of us be friends with you like we've been *trying* to do, this wouldn't have happened."

I feel awful and try to find the right words to tell her so, but they stick in my throat.

"But no," she says. "You had to be an ice queen and go your own way and now I have to work with you knowing you know what my boyfriend's O face looks like."

"I—I know."

The ice queen thing—it's not like I've never heard it before, but it still hurts.

She's not saying anything I don't know.

I'm *that* coworker.

The one who isn't really a very good "team player."

The one who isn't really a "people person."

Or, to put it the way Darren did when he broke off our three-year relationship last year, I'm *unknowable. A black box,* he said. *I kept waiting for you to open up to me, but now I know it's never going to happen.*

I've realized he was right, and since then, I've vowed to be better. Any armchair psychologist could tell you I'm closed off because my dad proved himself so untrustworthy in every possible way, but that easy assessment doesn't mean it's simple to fix.

"I meant what I said about giving notice," I say. "You don't have to work with me, I'll move on."

She throws her arms in the air. "Have you heard *anything* I just said? You are *not* giving notice. No notice!" She buries her face in her hands. "Oh, Lucy, *what* am I going to do with you?"

"Fire me?" I suggest. Again.

"I'm not firing you," she says.

"But I—"

I can't, I think.

I can't come to work knowing that within a day or so, everyone at work will know the story of what happened. How I stood up, all soft and eager and vulnerable, with my feelings showing all over my face, and said, "How did you find me?" like the heroine of a romantic comedy, except I wasn't the heroine.

I was the comic relief.

Gennie's expression softens.

And now it looks an awful lot like pity, too.

I would so, so, so much rather she hated me.

"Listen. I totally get it if you need a little time. Maybe a leave of absence. Say, three weeks. Take some time off. Let both of us reset."

"Please just let me quit," I beg.

She shakes her head. "If you sucked at your job, I would. But you're the best I've got, and I'm not letting you go that easily."

"Thank you." My voice is small again, but at least steady.

"I won't let this get in the way of what's best for the team or the business," Gennie says. "And I know you won't, either."

I thank her for the three weeks leave of absence. For her generosity in not firing me. I apologize again, while she waves it off.

When I go, though, I take the box with me. The one with the contents of my desk.

I think, *I'm never coming back here.*

Need more? You can get MAKE ME WILDER now!

Go to geni.us/MakeMeWilder

CHAPTER 1

MIKA

Seeing my old college friend for the first time in five years? Five hundred and sixty-seven dollars for roundtrip airfare and an Uber to Rush Creek.

Seeing my old college friend for the first time in five years, without the fear of her hot older brother appearing around every corner? Priceless.

"I'm so excited you're here," says Rachel, squeezing my arm. "We're going to have so much fun."

"I can't wait." I grin back at her.

"We're going to have plenty of time for girl talk. I promise." Rachel's expression turns serious. "First, we need to talk about your email."

Oh God. I'd just had a series of miserable dates and sent an email to Rachel: *Rescue me from my bad decisions. Please!* Yes, it was a little dramatic, but it led to Rachel inviting me out to Rush Creek for a long weekend and me jumping at the chance, so it wasn't necessarily a bad thing.

"We have plenty of time for that. Right now I want to

find out more about your life here." My bad decisions are chronic. We don't need to dive into all of that yet.

"It's a little chaotic, but I love it. Brody's got four brothers and a sister, and sometimes it's a lot. Other times, it's like I didn't realize how much I was missing by growing up with only one sibling," says Rachel as she pours me a glass of Malbec. "Speaking of siblings, Connor will be so sorry he missed you. He's gone skiing with the guys for a week."

"That's a shame." I try my best to sound convincing, and I think I scrape by. A one-night stand with your best friend's brother is never a good idea, but this had been worse because of our connection. Like...we *knew* each other, even though we'd just met. Turns out that kind of connection is super rare, and I've remembered Connor Perez way more than I should have over the years. I shove the thought away and my voice brightens. "But all the more time for us to catch up, right?"

"I can't wait for you to get to know Brody." Rachel gestures toward the kitchen where Brody is cooking us dinner. That right there is enough to make me love him, then add in the fact that a) he's nice and b) he looks like the kind of guy who could lift a small car and barely break a sweat, and I'd say Rachel hit the jackpot with her fiancé. He and his brothers run an outdoor adventure company called Wilder Adventures and even though I'm not the outdoorsy type—I like hot running water too much—it seems like the perfect fit for him. "He seems great."

"He is great." Rachel laughs. "Is that arrogant? It sounds arrogant when I hear myself say it."

"If you didn't think he was amazing, I'd wonder what

the hell was wrong with you." I poke her in the shoulder. "I'm happy for you. You have the job, the guy, the kid. Hell, you even have a dog."

"That's Connor's dog, Nellie. We're watching her while Connor's away. She's super mellow and Justin loves her, so it's no trouble."

Justin is Brody's four-year-old son and Rachel's future stepson. He's in the kitchen right now, "helping" his daddy with dinner. Talk about things that make your heart grow two sizes. Seeing this big burly guy with his adorable little boy will do it.

"There's nothing cuter than a boy and his dog," I say.

"Truth." Rachel laughs. "Oh wait, you're talking about Justin? Because Brody's pretty cute with him, too."

"Obviously." I feign rolling my eyes. "Although didn't you tell me Brody had a reputation as a player before he met you? You're not convincing me. Just saying."

Rachel shrugs. "He had some bad boy tendencies, but we worked those out."

"Hey, Rach," calls Brody. "Want to come in here and stir the sauce? I'm going to read Justin a story and get him ready for bed."

"Yep, coming." Rachel jumps up off the couch and I follow her into the big open kitchen.

With Justin on one hip, Brody leans over to give Rachel a peck on the lips. Justin winds his hands around her neck and squeezes. I hang back and let out a contented sigh, because seeing my oldest friend this happy is amazing.

Brody gives Rachel specific instructions about stirring the spaghetti sauce and carries Justin out. Rachel waits until he's gone before leaning against the counter, crossing her arms and saying, "He's way too particular about his sauce."

I'm super impressed that it's homemade. "Prego is my friend," I say.

"I know, right? The Wilder men take their food very seriously, which is a good thing for me." Rachel laughs. "So, tell me about you while I'm not stirring this sauce. I've been worried about you since you sent that email. What's really going on with you?"

"You don't need to worry. I just had a string of bad dates and it really got me down. I mean, one guy brought his mother on our date. Who does that?" I roll my eyes and grin, because even I can see it's funny now. "I sent that email to you in a moment of what-the-hell-am-I-even doing-with-my-life?"

"Okay, you should not be the one questioning yourself in that scenario," Rachel says. "Trust me."

"Possibly. But the good thing about reaching new lows is I've made a pact with myself not to get involved with anyone who's not ready to get serious. It cuts down on dating and going out, but that's not a bad thing. My job has been nuts the past six months. In other words, you have Justin and Brody, and I have corporate law." I grimace and shake my head. "That's pathetic, right?"

"Not at all. Jobs have a way of taking over your life."

"That's the truth. Sometimes I wonder if this is all there is, you know? I barely have time to go to the gym."

"I hate to break it to you, but you didn't go to the gym when you had time." Rachel raises an eyebrow and gives me a knowing look, but her tone is gentle when she adds,

"That said, it's never too late to make a change. I mean, look at me."

Rachel left her job as a librarian to sell sex toys and she's also a certified sex therapist. I think this is all kinds of awesome, but I can't see myself talking about sex toys without turning fifty shades of red.

"You're doing great. I don't know." I shrug. "Maybe I'll start looking around when I get home. Put some feelers out and see what else is out there."

"You could always start doing some of your art stuff again?" Rachel gives me a hopeful look.

"Hmmm. Maybe." I don't want to talk about my art, so I spin around and point to the cabinets, saying, "Where would I find a water glass in here? I'm drinking this wine like it's grape juice! I actually want to make it through dinner."

Rachel points to a cabinet behind me. As I turn to grab a glass, my gaze falls to a small, framed print of the night sky with the caption *Welcome to the World, Baby Sis*. I lean over to study it and say, "This is cool. What is it?"

Rachel slides up next to me and picks it up. "Connor got me this for my birthday. It's the star map from the night I was born. Pretty cool, right?"

"Very cool, and really thoughtful." The Connor I met was an unapologetic goofball—which was what attracted me to him in the first place—but he's sweet, as well? That combination could give my resolve a workout.

"I really do wish he was here." Rachel's sigh jerks me from my food-induced fantasies. "I'd love for you two to get to know each other a little more."

Connor and I got to know each other more than you'd like to think about, I almost tell her. The memory sends a little jolt to my low belly. "Yeah, I'd love that too." It's easy to be generous when no follow-through is required.

"Oh well. Maybe next time." Rachel brightens. "You're still up for the Rent-an-Elf thing tomorrow, right? It's a fundraiser—well, actually they call it a *fun*-raiser—that benefits American Heart Association's Go Red for Women movement. It's actually a lot of fun, so it lives up to its name. People bid on elf services, like wrapping gifts, decorating, even baking cookies. I promise you won't have to bake anything, though."

I snort. "No one wants that. Unless a local team needs chocolate chip hockey pucks, *then* I'm your girl. And yes, I'm in. This trip is kicking off the Christmas season for me, so whatever festive activities you've got on, sign me up."

"Rent-an-Elf is a Rush Creek tradition. I think you'll love—" Rachel pauses as a door slams in the living room. "What on earth?"

She spins on her heel and heads back to the living room, and I follow. I'm a few steps behind so it takes me a minute to register what's happening. But when I do, my heart pounds like a bass drum.

Standing in the middle of the living room, receiving enthusiastic licks and butt wiggles from Nellie, is Connor Perez. Connor Perez—who's supposed to be off on a ski holiday—is here. In the flesh.

Rachel hugs him and from the snippets of conversation I hear over the thrumming of my heart, it sounds like he's back to stay.

CHAPTER 2
CONNOR

My dog Nellie shoves her nose in my crotch, Rachel wraps me in a hug, and I catch Brody's quizzical expression over her shoulder. Rachel steps back, and it's clear that both she and Brody are waiting to find out what I'm doing back here in Rush Creek when I'm supposed to be cruising down black diamond runs in Utah.

"What the hell, Connor? Did you take a wrong turn on the way to Alta?" Brody demands. It's one of our favorite ski resorts.

I shake my head. "I was standing in the boarding line at the airport when I got a text from my buddy that his family screwed up and double-booked the chalet. We're gonna go in February instead. He'd already rebooked his flight. I rebooked mine, too."

I try not to sound as severely bummed as I am, because my family and friends don't need to know how badly I wanted to get out of Rush Creek—and away from the traditional Wilder-Perez Christmas festivities.

"That sucks."

Brody can always be counted on to at least read my body language, even if he doesn't necessarily share my feelings on the subject of Wilder Christmases. In old times, Brody probably would have been on this trip with me, but now that he's with Rachel and deep into Dadland, there's no chance of that.

They're all staring at me, waiting for my response, and I do what any decent man should do in this situation: I lie.

"Nah," I say. "This way I get my ski trip *and* Christmas with the family."

"Awww," Rachel says. I'm pretty sure I've sold it. Then I catch Brody's raised eyebrow.

Don't get me wrong: I love my family, especially my sister and Brody, and I love the happy fray that goes along with hanging out with the Wilders. But lately I feel like the odd man out. Everyone's paired off—well, not *everyone*, because they'll hold the Olympic luge event in the underworld before the youngest Wilder brother settles down—but almost everyone. And there's just so much *togetherness* at the holidays. Sometimes it can be too much for a bachelor to take. I was looking forward to escaping to the slopes with a college buddy and wingman, burning up the slopes during the day and getting my flirt on in the evenings.

The universe gave me a giant middle finger and a big fat nope on that one. Now I'm smack in the middle of the kind of gathering I'd been hoping to avoid this holiday season.

Rachel throws herself into my arms and gives me another huge hug. "Well," she says. "I'm sorry your plans fell through, but I'm super, super glad you're here! I was so bummed you were going to miss Mika, and now you won't!"

Mika.

Wait.

What are the chances...?

I pull away from my sister. My gaze follows hers across the room and lands on a familiar face.

No.

Oh, *come* on, universe, you've got to be kidding me.

It's Mika Radcliffe, Rachel's college roommate and best friend.

She's one hundred percent as absolutely gorgeous as I remember—dark-haired, dark-eyed, with the prettiest, smoothest skin I've ever seen and a petite body with slim curves I remember all too vividly under my hands.

The last time I saw her, when she and Rachel were in college, she was walking away without a backward glance.

Before that, she was under me in a tent at a music festival.

"Connor." Rachel's voice brims with delight. "You remember Mika, right? And Mika, you remember Connor?"

I give myself a mental high five for being able to meet her eyes.

"Hi, Mika." I try my best not to sound like I've seen her in her super-sexy pink lace underwear, that I know exactly how eager and responsive she is to the right touch. That I still think about it... way more than I'd like to admit.

Her gaze skips away from mine first, and yeah—that's about right. "Hi, Connor." Her voice has changed. It's the tiniest bit husky, like she's already anticipating...

Connor Perez, don't you dare.

Abruptly, I come to my senses, and, shit, this couldn't be

any more uncomfortable. Now we're standing more or less face-to-face, surrounded by a roomful of friends and family, meeting for the first time since we walked away from each other. I have to say something, or it will get way more awkward.

"It's, um, great to see you again." Brilliant, Connor.

"You too."

"How have you... been?"

The urge to bury my face in my hands is strong, but I'm somewhat cheered by the fact that Mika's cheeks are pinking up. She's as uncomfortable as I am. Also, blushing is *adorable* on her. She did it right before I kissed her. In fact, that was probably the reason I kissed her the first time. Although she wasn't blushing later, when we were half-undressed in her tent.

I need to stop thinking about that.

"I've been good! I've been doing the corporate law thing in upstate New York."

"Far from here." Then I want to smack myself across the mouth, because a) duh, New York state is far from Rush Creek, Oregon, and b) I'm not supposed to care.

"Yes." I think Mika's trying to hold back a smile. "Far from here."

"Connor!" Rachel breaks in. I'm wildly grateful to her for ending this painful exchange. "Since you're here, you can do the Rent-an-Elf fundraiser with Mika and Brody and me!"

Scratch the gratitude. My sister is the devil incarnate, and it's not even her fault, because she has no idea what a mess she's making.

I can't spend the day at the Rent-an-Elf Fundraiser with

Mika, because these past two minutes were awkward enough to end me.

And I definitely can't spend the day with Mika and Rachel, because if Rachel finds out I fooled around with her friend...

She knows nothing about our hookup, which Mika and I agreed was for the best. "You know we can never, ever tell your sister," Mika said, her swollen lips curving in a smile, right after we broke our first glorious, heated, I've-been-wanting-to-do-that-all-day kiss.

Rachel has never gotten wind of it. And I'm extra grateful for that now, because when Rachel and Brody got together, I gave Brody hell for hooking up with my sister. If Rachel and Brody knew that I'd done that, having messed around with Rachel's best friend...?

They would never stop giving me shit.

I open my mouth to launch a million excuses for why I can't be at the fundraiser tomorrow, then realize nothing I say will be credible, given that I was supposed to be on the ski slopes all day.

Rachel watches me with wide, little-sister, joyful eyes, while Brody glares in a way that clearly says, *I will break you if you disappoint my girl.*

I hazard a look at Mika. Her (beautiful) gaze reflects my own terror.

And there is nothing—absolutely nothing—I can do, other than to say, "That sounds like fun."

Mika closes her eyes, Rachel beams, and Brody gives a small, tight nod that says I bought myself another few days of life.

My stomach lands on the floor with a thud.

At the earliest possible convenience, I must remind Mika that Rachel can never find out what happened.

CHAPTER 3

MIKA

I'm not sure if it's the too-loud Christmas music, the flurry of activity or the adults dressed as actual elves—complete with green pointy shoes—that make me feel like I've stepped through the Looking Glass, but Elf Central is bananas. People dressed as elves run around, madly matching volunteers with requests for help. When Rachel grabs my arm and says, "Isn't this great?" I'm too overwhelmed to do anything but nod and smile.

Not that she's deterred. She tugs me further into the melee, beelining toward two women, one with a baby strapped to her front. Even from five steps away I can see the baby's sleeping, which is #momgoals as far as I can tell. If a baby can sleep through this chaos, I assume it can sleep through anything.

When Rachel introduces me to Lucy and Mari, her future sisters-in-law, the first thing Mari says is, "Please don't be offended if I forget your name in five minutes. I've slept about six minutes in the past two days because this one hasn't been sleeping, and if she's awake, we're all awake."

Mari wraps her hands around the baby's little bottom, and when she smiles I can see the tiny lines around her eyes. I smile in reply and say, "She looks like a great sleeper to me."

"I know, right?" Mari rolls her eyes. "She could sleep through a rave, but in her crib? Not so much."

"Mari and Kane are trying to get Zara on a schedule," Rachel says. "They're determined she's going to have an actual bedtime."

"Schedule, schmedule." Lucy grins. "Sooner or later you realize it's futile."

Mari says something about swaddling, and I tune them out. I love a cute baby as much as the next person, but my knowledge of small people is pretty much zero. Besides, there's a big person I'm more concerned with right now.

Speaking of sleeplessness.

I'm not saying thinking about Connor Perez kept me up last night, but every time I closed my eyes, there he was. Not literally, because that would be weird—although maybe not entirely unwelcome—but I just kept *seeing* him. His large strong hands. Those broad sturdy shoulders. Those muscular thighs and firm, tight ass. He was a fine specimen back in college, and he's grown into a handsome rugged man and that's almost as disconcerting as the sheer attraction to him I felt last night. I don't know why I expected him to be the same person he was. I'm not the same person I was. I guess I didn't expect him to be so virile. Or for me to respond to him like I did. Like our one night together was minutes ago, not years, and I'm eager for round two.

Or maybe round one, given that we only made it to point-five? Our tent sexcapades didn't result in actual sex, thanks to the untimely return of my friend, Shelly. But it was enough of a preview to make me wonder if Connor's stubble on my thighs would feel as good as it did on my nipples, and if that mouth—

I'm wrenched from veering into any X-rated thoughts by a firm hand on my arm. When I turn to look, a fifty-something blonde woman dressed as an elf says, "Come on now. Busy elves are happy elves. Let's get you a job to do. How do you feel about wrapping gifts?"

"Um, fine." My answer hardly matters because the elf pulls me along after her. I give a helpless look at Lucy, Mari, and Rachel who smile and wave, but none of them move to rescue me. Jerks. I wave at Rachel to come with me because at least we can hang out while wrapping gifts, but as she starts toward me, another elf whisks her in the opposite direction.

Okay, solo gift wrapping it is. I turn back to the elf to ask her where we're going. Just then she releases me and reaches out to grab Connor's flannel-clad arm, giving him the same spiel she gave me. The deep red of his shirt barely makes the cut for the red we're all wearing today in honor of Go Red for Women, but the color matches the ruddy flush of his cheeks. His hair still has flecks of snow in it, too, so he's obviously just arrived, but I feel like I conjured him up from my slightly inappropriate thoughts earlier.

He glances at me and his eyes widen. "Mika? Are we on elf duty together?"

"Yep. Gift wrapping apparently." I smile and shrug. I'm no professional-grade gift wrapper, but at least it's not baking. This is going to be awkward enough without me fumbling to find the right measuring spoon.

Connor shakes his head and says to the elf, "You know, I really think I'd be better at shoveling snow or something. Maybe I can deliver Christmas trees?"

His tone is hopeful, but the elf's grip on his arm is firm. "You'll have a chance to volunteer at more than one station, but this morning we're going to send the two of you on a gift-wrapping mission. It's just a short walk from here."

"I don't think that's a great idea," Connor says.

My stomach sinks. I get that this is awkward, but come on. I'm not Medusa. He's not going to turn to stone if we spend an hour together.

"It's just that I'm pretty sure a toddler could do a better job gift wrapping than me." Connor sounds dejected. "You don't know how bad my wrapping is. I use gift bags in my own life because it's cheaper than all the tape I go through."

I can't help laughing. Partly because I can picture it, but also partly because my stomach is suddenly back where it belongs. He wasn't avoiding me, just the task.

He turns around and gives me a look that would be a growl if it made a sound.

"I've got you. Don't worry." I grin at him, and his growly look morphs into a resigned eye roll. But I'm almost positive I see the corner of his mouth tick up, which feels like a win.

I slow down and linger behind Connor and the elf for a second, pulling my phone out of my pocket to snap a furtive photo of Connor's backside. Pulling up my message thread to my friend Evie back in Enita Springs, I attach the photo and type: *Admiring the scenery.*

Evie's response is immediate—a bunch of emojis followed by a string of question marks. Then she types: *Who's that? Anyone I should know?*

I grin at my phone, but before I can reply, I glance up and find Connor's eyes trained on me. It's nothing, just a glance, but I can't help feeling like a kid caught peeking at her Christmas presents.

Whatever I was going to say is gone, erased by the flush on my cheeks and the quickening of my pulse. Connor is not going to be beneath my Christmas tree this year, so there will be no unwrapping. Of any kind. He's off limits. Period.

To Evie I text: *Just a cute guy.*

Then I turn to follow him and the elf toward our gift-wrapping destination. Connor might suck at our task, but I can't help feeling like I'm the one who's going to be tied in knots today.

CHAPTER 4

CONNOR

Because the universe is not done messing with me, the "gift wrapping destination" is the Rush Creek Bakery, and the gifts in question belong to its proprietor, Nan. Nan is Rush Creek's most beloved busybody and resident bigmouth, and there is zero chance that she will not comment on my arrival at her bakery with a pretty woman in tow.

And Mika is even prettier this morning than she was last night. I can't stop sneaking peeks. She's wearing a pair of dark skinny jeans and a scoop-necked red top that bares soft-looking skin. Her long black hair is hanging down her back today, too, and I want to run my fingers through it.

"Connor Perez!" Nan exclaims as the door swings shut behind us. She dusts off her hands on her apron. Flour surrounds Nan in a cloud and follows her wherever she goes, the way dirt wafts around Pigpen in the old Charlie Brown cartoon. "Are you my elf? And who is your girlfriend?"

Aaaaaaaugh!

"Not his girlfriend," Mika says helpfully—if a little too quickly and firmly for my tastes. "I'm Rachel's friend Mika."

"Nan." She extends a hand, which Mika takes. Nan swings a look my way. "It would serve your sister right if you took up with *her* best friend, wouldn't it?"

Toooo close for comfort.

I blink innocently. "But I would never, ever do something like that. Especially not for revenge."

Nan squints at me. "Connor Perez, I've known you since you were little, so don't give me that virtuous BS. Watch out for this one," she tells Mika.

"Noted," Mika says, smiling at Nan. "And, yes, we're your wrapping elves. Point us to where you need us."

Nan leads us to a table near the back and leaves us standing there, staring at the rolls of wrapping paper. She brings out a platter of cookies big enough to spoil lunch *and* dinner. Mika's eyes meet mine, and we both grab for chocolate chip cookies at the same time, our fingers brushing as we do. I take a huge bite—Nan's cookies are the *best*—and Mika does the same, with gusto and a small hum of approval. I'm reminded that Mika was a hungry, eager participant the night we were together.

I loved that about her.

Nan begins carrying out tote bags filled with more rolls of shiny paper and bright ribbons, which she piles on the table and all around us. My heart sinks. The only thing I suck at more than tape and paper is ribbon.

Mika is undaunted, cheerfully oohing over everything Nan brings out.

Until the gifts start arriving.

"Menstrual cup?" Mika whispers, after Nan deposits something blue and silicone on the table between us.

I raise my eyebrows. "Wouldn't that make an awkward Christmas gift?"

"I don't know? My aunt once gave me reusable pantyliners." She tugs the package closer. "Oh," she says, the corner of her mouth turning up. "It's a collapsible kitchen funnel."

Our sighs of relief are audible.

The relief turns out to be premature when Nan comes back and sets several more items down.

I seriously consider fleeing before Mika realizes what's sitting in front of us—but it's too late. Her eyes get huge. Though not quite as huge as the shrink-wrapped, hot pink, eight-inch, silicone-molded penis. And that's just one of several items in the same vein—all obviously purchased at one of Rachel's parties—which I do *not* need to think about Nan attending.

My sister used to be a librarian, until she discovered that her true love in life was helping women find their sexual mojo. Now she's a sex therapist and purveyor of high-end sex toys.

"That's—" Mika says. Her eyes come up and find mine, full of amusement and something... else. Curiosity maybe? Mika's cheeks shade toward the color of the toy on the table. My cock, not to be outdone by Mr. Hot Pink, stirs to life.

"Going to be hard to wrap," she finishes, and reaches for a roll of gift paper.

Nan, utterly unselfconscious—more power to her—is still bustling between the back room and our table, piling on the goods. There is one other occupied table in the bakery, but the couple is deep in conversation—also blessedly unaware of our dirty Christmas duties.

I look back at the table, at the motley collection of unidentifiable kitchen items, intimacy aids, compression stockings, and oddly shaped kids' toys. "Everything here is hard to wrap," I say with a groan.

"Here. This one should be easy." She hands me a book.

"*Sixteen Ways to Love Yourself*," I read. "Eight of which are on this table," I quip.

Mika snort-laughs. She points to the book. "You can wrap that, right?"

"Your faith is touching." I grab a roll of bright red wrapping paper with snow people...

Having sex in a variety of positions.

Seriously, universe? Uncle! Okay?

I set a roll of gift wrap on the table and line up the book to measure out how much paper I need. I have to turn the book side-over-side to figure out where to cut, and the gift wrap fights back, wrinkling and tearing.

I sneak a look at Mika. Her fingers fly over the paper and tape, quick, careful, and precise, and I think of the way they felt on my body, warm, soft, generous. Then she pulls out a spool of red ribbon, and all I can think about is the tiny pink satin bow on her lace bra, tucked like a delicious secret between perfect-handful breasts. And the way her skin felt under my tongue.

Focus, Connor!

In the time it's taken me to cut the piece of wrapping paper and ogle Mika's competent fingers, she has neatly wrestled Mr. Hot Pink into a silver condom—and wrapped three other items.

A piece of tape sticks to me and itself. I wrestle it off and try again.

"You weren't lying," she says, watching me struggle to create a semi-straight seam and lay tape down on it. "You know what helps? Fold over the edge." She shows me.

She's right. It does help. I get that seam to look pretty damn good.

Next up: the end folds. Mine always end up being more like end wrinkles.

"Here."

The next thing I know, she's tucked under my arm, her body close to mine. She's warm and soft and my reaction is instant—full body tingles and a surge of blood south that catches me off guard. She puts her hands over mine and guides my hands on the wrapping paper. Her fingers are nimble and sure, just like I remembered, and I make a sound that has nothing to do with gratitude.

She half turns to look at me, startled, and I know there's no way she can't see how much the contact has affected me. Her eyes get wide, and her pupils flare.

She drops my hands and steps away.

"I'm sorry," she says. "That was—it was a bad idea then, and it's a bad idea now."

I release a held breath and nod.

As bummed as I am to hear that verdict from her, I know she's right. There's still the Rachel-would-kill-me and-Brody-would-bury-the-body factor.

"Yeah," I say. "About that. I need to ask you a favor. What happened—back then—I know it's been years, but I need you not to say anything to Rachel about it. I may or may not have given her absolute hell when she got together with Brody, about the fact that he was my friend, and they didn't tell me what was going on..."

A slow grin spreads over Mika's face.

"You find the thought of my death funny." I raise my eyebrows.

"You have to admit, that's pretty funny."

"Please. Don't tell her."

She smirks at me. "I don't owe you anything," she says. "If I remember correctly, you *owe* me."

"I owe you..." I drag the words out, because I'm genuinely confused.

Realization slowly dawns.

"Oh," I say. "Oh, *that*."

"Yeah," she says. "My missing orgasm."

Now I turn pink—or at least it feels that way from the heat in my face. And, well, everywhere. Thinking about Mika's missing orgasm—or more exactly, about the orgasm I would like to *find* for her—is making me glad the table is between us.

Actually, I hate the table. I want to overturn it, toss it out of the way, and make up for lost time.

And owed orgasms.

"I don't like to be in debt to anyone."

"No?" I can tell she's holding back a smile, her lips quirking despite her best effort.

I shake my head, meeting her curious gaze steadily. "I *always* repay what I owe."

She bites her lip. Her mouth is soft, peachy-pink, and lush. I drag my eyes back to hers.

I nod. "Mmm-hmm. With interest."

CHAPTER 5

MIKA

Oh. My.

Is that a proposition? My lady parts definitely think so. I swear to God, my nipples have the high beams on so bright it's amazing Connor isn't blinded by them.

Although to be fair, he's not looking at my chest. He's looking at my eyes and there's a heat in his gaze that's unmistakable. Which makes the rest of my body hum. All I would have to do is lean across this table and...

"Good to know." My voice comes out a bit strangled, which is enough to wrench me back to reality. When I speak again, I sound almost prim. "I'll take your word for it."

"I have more than my word to offer. Just saying." That line would sound sleazy coming from anyone but Connor. With a shrug and an easy grin, he makes it work.

It's an adorable combination.

Not that I'm thinking Connor is adorable. Or sexy. Or

appealing in any kind of sexual way. With my history of choosing the wrong guys, Connor would be the absolute wrongest, and not only because he's Rachel's younger brother, but because he lives on the opposite side of the country. Talk about distant and unavailable! I don't even know if he has a proper job.

I can't help asking. "I don't know what you do for a living these days. I feel like Rachel told me and I forgot."

If Connor thinks my segue is weird, he doesn't let on. "I'm a forest ranger, which basically means I do a lot of planting, working with trees, fire prevention, and even some community education programs."

And now I'm imagining him shirtless with an axe.

"Do you like it?" I ask as I pick up another sex toy to wrap. Speaking of imagining Connor shirtless. God help me.

"Yeah, it's great. Every day is different, which is what I like about it." Connor picks up a package of baby onesies to wrap. I mentally pat myself on the back for only spending a few seconds imagining his big hands wrapped around a tiny baby. Any longer and my ovaries would probably explode. "What about you? What are you doing these days?"

"I'm a corporate lawyer in Rochester." I make a face. "It's okay. Being a lawyer isn't as exciting as *Suits* would have you believe."

Connor laughs. "If you don't love it, why not do something else? If I remember correctly, you're an amazing artist. You painted everyone's faces at that music festival and it was so cool."

My face flushes with pleasure. Connor remembers that about me because it's something very few people even know about me back in Enita Springs. But I shake my head, saying, "My art was just for fun."

Corporate law isn't the most exciting job, but it keeps my family off my back. The one time in high school I even alluded to wanting to take my art more seriously, my mother immediately signed me up for extra SAT prep sessions. As if higher test scores would squelch my artistic desires.

Connor doesn't get to respond because Nan comes over bearing a tray of cake slices. We've barely made a dent in the chocolate chip cookies she left, but she sets down her tray with a flourish and says, "I need you two to do me a favor."

"Does that favor involve this cake?" Connor asks with a grin. "Because if so, I'm all in."

"Yup. I'm branching out into cakes, finally. And this is not just any cake. It's my better-than-sex cake. I'm not going to call it that if it's a misnomer, so I need you to tell me if it is. Better than sex, I mean."

"I mean, if a cake is better than sex you're probably having the wrong kind of sex," Connor says. Then he looks at me and says, "Am I right?'"

Why? Why is everything about this day reminding me how long it's been since I've had good sex?

"Probably." My voice has that strangled sound to it again.

"Good point," says Nan. "Maybe I should call it my better-than-Robert-Redford cake."

I resist saying that Robert Redford is a bit past his prime because Nan looks genuinely worried about this.

"I'll tell you what. Leave it with us and we'll taste test for you. Right, Mika?"

Oh, the sound of my name coming out of Connor's mouth is better than Robert Redford, for sure.

"I'm always up for some cake," I say.

"Okay. Let me know what you think and don't hold back," says Nan. "I'm done letting Carol's Cake Shop win best cake every year."

Someone calls her name and she turns away, leaving the cake beside the pile of gifts we've barely made a dent in. I feel my familiar sense of responsibility kick in and say, "How about we reward ourselves with cake for wrapping ten more presents each?"

"Ten?" Connor's eyes widen, and he looks mildly terrified.

"Twenty then? We need to make a dent in this pile."

"What have you got against immediate gratification?" Connor asks, raising his eyebrows.

I swallow hard because, yes, my mind went there. Again. "Nothing at all. But this pile is still massive and I, for one, could use some motivation to get through it."

"You just want to show off your superior wrapping skills."

"If you've got it, flaunt it." I laugh and mimic cutting motions with the scissors.

But I can't help noticing that Connor's eyes aren't on the scissors at all. They're raking down my body in appreciation. It makes me feel powerful. And sexy. It doesn't hurt that every time I meet Connor's gaze as we're wrapping our ten gifts, he's smiling at me or laughing at himself. He's just so... easy. Easy to be around. Easy in his own skin. Easy on the eyes. That was what first attracted me to him all those years ago, and it still holds, dammit.

If he were a random guy, I might consider breaking my own rules for the weekend, past patterns be damned. But Connor is Rachel's brother and I don't keep things from my friends. I definitely don't keep the same thing from the same friend twice. Plus, I'm done with unavailable guys. Aren't I?

Connor picks up a massive plastic tower from the floor and sets it on the table. "This one is for after cake. No way I can do this one without a sugar rush."

"Uh, not to be rude, but I'm not sure a sugar rush is going to help with that one." I laugh because Connor definitely did not undersell his wrapping ability. He's terrible, and a giant plastic toddler-toy may just break him.

"Well, it can't hurt." Connor turns toward the cake and grabs a piece, sliding it onto a red napkin. "What do you say to a bite of better-than-sex cake?"

"Just a bite?" I'm playing with fire, but I can't seem to help myself.

"You know what they say. Don't bite off more than you can chew." Connor raises his eyebrows. It feels like a dare.

"Funny. I thought they said to use more tongue than teeth." My eyes widen and I feel my face flush because I can't believe I said that. I add quickly, "I mean for the frosting. To taste the frosting."

Connor's face is flushed, too, I think, but he just holds the piece of cake out to me and says, "Well, by all means, go ahead."

Oh my God. What am I doing? Not him. Not him. Not him. Maybe if I keep reminding myself, it will sink in.

I lean over and take a bite of Nan's cake. I don't know what I expected from a better-than-sex cake, but this is phenomenal. The cake is super moist and gooey chocolate with caramel undertones and the frosting is creamy toffee. I can't help moaning, because it's that good.

"Um, okay, I see where the name comes from now," says Connor.

His voice is strained and I look up at him. If I thought his gaze was heated before...

I quickly look away and swallow saying, "Oh my God, you have to try it. It may actually be good enough to help you wrap that gift after all."

"That would be one hell of a cake." Connor pops the rest of the piece in his mouth, and I watch his face as he chews slowly. When the full impact of the flavor hits, his eyes flutter. A low growl escapes his throat as he says, "Holy shit."

I laugh. "I know, right?"

"I'm not going to say this is better than sex, but it's better than Robert Redford, definitely," says Connor.

"Completely agree. I've never had cake like this before."

"We need to tell Nan to add this to her regular rotation. It's a winner." Connor runs his tongue over his teeth and grins at me. He reaches a hand out. "You have a little bit of frosting here."

He wipes at the corner of my lip with his thumb. It's a featherlight touch, but the nerve endings in my lips tingle, and it's all I can do to keep myself from biting his thumb or, worse, sucking on it. I turn away and toward the table, my movements jerky as I say, "Thanks. So, how are we going to tackle this thing then?"

If Connor notices my reaction, he's kind enough to ignore it. He looks at the toy and says, "I say we go at it with paper and tape and hope for the best."

I'm too frazzled to think of a better way, so I grab the wrapping paper and start winding it around the toy. Connor slaps on tape randomly, closing up gaps I leave, and we're full on belly laughing by the time he smacks the last piece on top.

"Ta da," he says with a flourish. "It's a masterpiece."

"I think the toddler this is intended for could probably have done a better job." I laugh and shake my head.

"Nope. It's ready for a ribbon. It's perfectly imperfect." Connor steps back and crosses his arms over his chest. "That's my story and I'm sticking to it."

"Is it?" I eye up the uneven paper and excess tape. It's far from perfect, but I love Connor's devil-may-care attitude. Left to my own devices, I'd rip the wrapping paper off and start over again, smoothing down all of the edges and hiding as much of the tape as I could.

"You don't think so?" Doubt flickers over Connor's features.

"No. I mean, it's great. I love it, actually."

I'm not lying. The more I look at it, the more I love it because it's so quintessentially Connor. He's gloriousy messy but careful where it counts, like taping down the corners and double wrapping over the top so the point doesn't break through. I wonder if he'd be like that as a lover? From what I remember, the answer is a resounding yes. He may not have given me an orgasm, but he gave me *plenty* to fantasize about afterward, and the fact that we were interrupted wasn't his fault. A warmth blooms in my stomach, but I tamp it down.

I'm not going there. I'm not doing this to myself again. The sooner my body gets the memo, the better.

CHAPTER 6
CONNOR

When the wrapping's done, Mika and I head back to Elf Central together. As soon as we step inside, we're accosted by a harried elf-costumed coordinator.

"Can you two take another job?" she demands.

Mika and I exchange a quick glance. Her expression's uncertain, and I realize she's not sure whether I want us to keep working together.

Well, fuck that. "Absolutely," I tell the coordinator, and am rewarded by a full-on Mika smile.

"It's a light-stringing job. Do you have transportation? It's on site and it's outside of town, so you'll need to be able to get yourselves there." She consults her clipboard and rattles off an address that sounds vaguely familiar.

"We could go in my truck." It's my turn to check in with Mika, raising my eyebrows to make sure she's comfortable with that, and getting a grin and a nod back.

"You don't have a particular time you have to be done

by, do you?" the coordinator asks. "This one might take you a while."

"Oh, we're very efficient," I tell her.

She beams. "Excellent!"

Fifteen minutes later, Mika and I pull into a neighborhood just outside of town.

"Oh, *no*," I say, as my brain resolves the address we've been given and I put two and two together.

"What?"

"It's—okay, so you know how for some people, Christmas decorating is more than a hobby?"

"Uh... yeah?"

"This is one of those houses. You know, glow in the sky, nativity scenes *and* Santa's sleigh with all eight reindeer, a million lights plus a million inflatables and weird plastic doohickeys left over from the 1970s?"

"Oh, *shit*," Mika says. "So that's why she asked if we had anywhere we needed to be anytime soon."

We hop down from the truck and introduce ourselves to the home's owners, Rebecca and Wallace Merrithrift. They're an older couple—I'd guess pushing eighty—and they're beside themselves with excitement and gratitude at seeing us. They keep saying what an amazing fundraiser Rent-an-Elf is, and how great it is that in addition to everything else, the donations are going to such a great cause— early detection of heart attack and stroke in women.

I couldn't agree with them more. My abuelita had a mild heart attack last summer, and thanks to a Go Red for Women info sheet her physician had given her, she knew that even though she didn't have chest pain, the nausea and discomfort in her neck and arms were trying to tell her something important. She called my mom, we got her to the ER, and they were able to treat her immediately. One surgery later, she's fine. Well. Maybe a little grumpy about the whole eating-better thing...

Rebecca and Wallace are bossy as shit, unlocking and throwing open the enormous shed that houses their glow-in-the-sky Christmas collection, then telling us exactly where everything needs to go.

We inflate the Grinch, Santa, and Christmas Yoda with electric pumps, arrange plastic sheep and donkeys, and string lights, as Rebecca and Wallace supervise, calling out instructions and corrections.

"Let me help with that," I tell Mika. She's on a way-too-rickety ladder, stringing lights in one of the old trees that decks the front of the property. I forego the ladder and climb the tree—thank you, eight-year-old self—and start helping her with the parts that are harder to reach so she won't have to lean so far out.

"Can you grab this?" she asks.

I work my way around the tree to take the end of the string from her and discover that I've inadvertently tangled both of us in a length of lights. "Whoops," I say. "Hold still."

I have to lean into her to unwrap the lights from around the back of the ladder. This brings our faces together. Her long, dark lashes flutter. Her skin, this close, looks like satin, and without meaning to, I raise my hand to smooth my fingers over the curve of her cheek. It's as soft as I remember, and heat and hunger pool in my chest. Her breath catches, and my eyes drop to her mouth, glossy and inviting. I slip my hand behind her head and draw her toward me, a small gasp escaping her lips as I lean in.

"Those are the wrong lights!" Rebecca calls from below.

I startle and grab the trunk to keep from tumbling out of the tree. My other hand is still in Mika's hair, as her mouth drops open in panic and she grabs a handful of my shirt. With a valiant effort, we manage to stabilize ourselves before either of us fall. We let out twin huffs of relief—and then start laughing. Mika's face is rosy pink, her eyes shining, and I take a deep breath, wanting desperately to reach for her again.

Rebecca appears at the base of the ladder. "The multi-color lights go in this tree. The blue LED ones go in that one." Rebecca points.

The look Mika gives me as we pull apart is full of promise and intent. We may have been interrupted, that look says, but we're not done. And I'm more than okay with that.

"Okay!" Mika calls. "Will do!"

I wink at her and we both muffle our laughter.

"I guess we're unstringing this tree," I say.

"Looks like it," she says, through giggles.

Neither of us comments on what almost happened, but the not-doneness hovers in the air between us, delicious and tempting. My head is full of what-happens-nexts, all of which involve me kissing Mika until she makes that tantalizing sound she unveiled for the better-than-sex cake.

We switch the lights to follow Rebecca's instructions, then climb down. As soon as our feet are on solid ground, I say what I've needed to say all day.

"Hey. I owe you a *real* apology. Not just for the missing orgasm, although that, too, but for what a dickwad I was the next day."

Mika bites her lip. "You were, kinda." There's no heat in her voice, and I know her well enough by now to see the smile she's holding back.

I shuffle from one foot to the other. "This isn't an excuse —there's no excuse—but I didn't know how to get back to where we were. Everything was amazing, and then your roommate stumbled in and passed out..."

Mika's almost-smile turns wry. "And it got super awkward."

I'm so relieved to hear her say it. "Yeah. The vibe was smashed to hell."

"We took that walk afterwards, but it was still weird. And I was thinking how much long distance sucks and that Rachel would flip if she knew I'd hooked up with you."

"Me too, on both counts. But I should have just *said* something. If I had any communication skills at all at that point in my life, I would have told you how totally great that day was and how amazing you felt to me—" My chest tightens at the memory.

"Yeah?" she asks, lighting up like a string of Christmas lights.

"Oh, God, yes. Kissing you..."

I lose my words. But I need them, so I dig deep.

"Kissing you wasn't like kissing anyone else. I hadn't wanted someone like that...ever. And it wasn't just because you're insanely hot..."

She gets a pleased little smile on her face that I can feel all the way down to the root of my rapidly hardening cock.

"I mean, it was definitely partly because of that," I add. "But it was also just how much fun we had at the festival. You were funny and smart and had it all together."

Her smile slips a bit. "I most definitely did *not* have it all together," she says.

"Well. It seemed like you did. Your bra and panties matched." I feel heat flare at the memory. "And your socks were that same pink."

She shakes her head. "Inside, I was a hot mess."

"Well. I cosign the *hot* part, but I will never agree to *mess*. You've seen my gift-wrapping skills. Or should I say lack of gift-wrapping skills?"

She chuckles, and something expands, hot and bright, in my chest. She's so fucking pretty. And—all the other things I said. Smart, funny—everything I've ever wanted with gift wrap and a tiny pink tease of a ribbon.

I'm going to kiss her. Again. Right now. And it's going to feel so good.

I take a step toward her.

I take a deep breath. This is the moment I didn't even know I've been waiting years for. But I don't want to wait another second to kiss her. I lean down.

Mika's phone rings.

CHAPTER 7

MIKA

It takes me three rings to hear my phone, even after Connor pulls back like I stung him. That's how wrapped up I am in this moment. In him. He was going to kiss me. I'm sure of it. And I not only wanted that kiss, I craved it.

I'm still craving it, so it's no wonder I'm breathless when I answer my phone without looking at the screen. "Hello?"

"Mika, hey." Rachel's voice is bubbly and bright on the other end of the line. "Where are you? I've been cleaning out someone's garage for the past hour and I hope you don't think I've abandoned you."

"No, no. It's fine. I'm fine." I force myself to mimic Rachel's tone. "I'm hanging Christmas lights for a really nice couple."

"Oh, great. Do you need a ride or anything? I can come get you? It's snowing pretty steadily here."

Shit, shit, shit. Two hours ago Connor asked me not to tell Rachel about the two of us, and even though it's perfectly legitimate that we could be hanging Christmas lights together and not lighting each other up, I say, "I'm fine. I think someone's coming to pick me up in a bit. I'll just meet you back at Elf Central."

"Okay, if you're sure. But if you get stuck, call me. I've been recruited to help paint someone's bedroom ceiling, but you know I wouldn't mind giving that a miss."

"Well, that sounds awful." I laugh.

"Exactly." I can hear someone call Rachel's name, and she says to me, "I've got to run, but seriously, call me if you get stuck."

"I will," I say, but she's already hung up.

"Thanks for not throwing me under the bus." Connor's voice is quiet. I feel like he wants to say more, but he doesn't.

"Yeah, of course. I said I wouldn't tell and I'm a woman of my word." I shrug like it's a given, but my own words sting like a papercut, because even though I'm the queen of reading things wrong, I'm sure Connor was about to kiss me before Rachel called. And I let myself get swept up in him enough to lie to my friend. Again. Not exactly being a woman of my word, is it? God, where are my loyalties? To one of my oldest friends or to a guy I've known for just a couple of days? Plus, I'm not doing this anymore, dammit! Best friend loyalties aside, hooking up with Connor is the emotional equivalent of wearing white pants with a black thong. In a rainstorm.

I open my mouth to respond to Connor when Rebecca calls from across the snowy yard, "Does anyone want a hot chocolate? It's got marshmallows."

I turn to see Rebecca carrying a tray of mugs and Wallace stepping gingerly behind her through the snow.

My first instinct is alarm. What if they fall? Connor must have the same thought, because he strides across the yard and takes the tray from Rebecca. "Thank you. That's really thoughtful of you."

I step up behind him, and he turns to hand me a mug of steamy hot chocolate. Our gloved fingers brush, and even through two layers of wool, I feel the heat there. I can see it in Connor's gaze, too, which makes me feel better. Maybe I'm not reading things wrong after all.

I take a sip of hot chocolate. It's creamy and warm, and I think I taste a pinch of cayenne pepper in there. "This is delicious."

"When the kids were younger, we'd make a day of putting up the outside Christmas decorations. The hot chocolate breaks were always my favorite part," says Wallace with a smile. "Becky used to make these salted caramel brownies, too, back before you could get salted caramel everything."

"Sorry, I don't do much baking anymore," says Rebecca. I have a feeling Wallace is the only one who can get away with calling her Becky.

"And ladders are *definitely* a thing of the past for us," Wallace says, "so we've had to find new decorating traditions. Rent-an-Elf has been such a blessing." They exchange glances filled equally with nostalgia and affection.

"Maybe just as well about the brownies," Connor says. "We had our fill of baked goods earlier. Before this, we were wrapping gifts at Rush Creek Bakery and Nan kept us well-supplied."

"Oh, I do love her baked goods," says Rebecca.

"She was branching out into cakes today. Be on the lookout for a better-than-Robert-Redford cake," says Connor with a meaningful glance at me.

My mind takes me back to the better-than-sex cake, and I feel my cheeks flush. A gulp of hot chocolate doesn't seem to help, so I blurt out, "Have you always had such a great collection of Christmas decorations?"

Wallace nods. "We built it up over time, of course, but I was always of the mind that there's no such thing as too much Christmas."

"You're still of that mind, dear," says Rebecca, placing a hand on Wallace's arm.

Oh my God, they are the cutest couple I've ever seen and my heart is expanding like a balloon right now.

"Well, all the kids are coming home this year. We have to give them something to put on that social media of theirs," says Wallace.

"Trust me, your house is always on social media," Connor says. "People come for miles to see your lights and decorations. I think Christmas Yoda got his own hashtag one year."

"That's a good thing," I add with a grin. "I'd hashtag Christmas Yoda."

"I probably would, too," says Rebecca. She laughs and continues, "Does that make me down with the kids?"

We all laugh, and I look up at the snow, letting it settle on my face. "It's beautiful here. I'm sure snow in Rush Creek is different from snow anywhere else."

"It's the fresh mountain air," says Rebecca. "Although speaking of snow, it's coming down pretty steadily now."

It is, and I know we should probably hit the road. But

I'm reluctant to leave this couple and their warm holiday spirit.

Connor nods and says, "We need to get back to Elf Central, but thank you for sharing your Christmas cheer with us."

"Thank you," Wallace says. "We could never have done this by ourselves and it means a lot that you came out to help."

"It was our pleasure," I say. "I hope you have a wonderful Christmas with your family."

"You two do the same," Rebecca says.

We exchange Merry Christmases, and Connor and I turn to begin trudging back to his truck through the snow. It's cold and the snow is definitely deeper than it was when we arrived. We probably should have left an hour ago. But then Connor takes my hand and squeezes it, and I think there's nowhere else I'd rather be. Snow and all.

CHAPTER 8
CONNOR

As we pull away from the Merrithrifts' house, I put on KXRC, which is currently playing all Christmas hits, all the time. Jingle Bell Rock is playing, and I sing along, totally butchering the lyrics.

Mika snickers.

"What?" I say, possibly a tiny bit more defensively than I meant to.

"I'm not laughing at you. I'm laughing with you! I totally love that you do that."

I almost swerve off the road. The "L" word, spoken in Mika's voice, does something abrupt and almost painful to my chest.

"Do what?" I ask cautiously.

"Sing along even when you have *no* idea what the words are. You did that at the Music Festival, the night we hooked up. I thought it was so cute. You just, I don't know, live in the moment, do what you want to do, don't give a shit what people think."

"Some people would say that's my worst trait," I say darkly.

"Well. They're wrong." She says it with so much certainty that for what might be the first time in my life, I actually believe that someone doesn't see me as the fuckup Perez sibling.

I'm so busy hanging onto her words that it takes me a minute to register how fast the snow's coming down.

Holy shit, it's snowing *hard*. And I grew up in these mountains, driving trucks with chains, so it's tough to stop me. But this isn't just snow, it's one hell of a squall.

"Yikes," Mika says.

"Seriously."

I make it maybe half a mile further on the winding mountain road before the snow whites out my windshield. I know I can't go any further without endangering our lives.

"I'm pulling over," I tell Mika.

"I support that."

I pull over and kill the engine. My heart's pounding, and it takes a lot to freak me out.

Or maybe my heart's pounding for another reason.

Here we are, alone in my truck, on a deserted road, tucked away from the world. It's almost Christmas, snow is falling, and the most beautiful woman in the world is sitting next to me.

"Was this in the weather prediction?" She bites her plump, delectable lip.

I shake my head. "But squalls aren't super unusual, this time of year. Shouldn't last too long? And hey—forest rangers are like boy scouts. We're *always* prepared."

She makes a humming sound.

"What?"

"You must know that's hot, Connor. Living in the moment, singing like no one's listening, *and* being an actual prepared adult man."

"Hot, huh?" I tease, raising an eyebrow. "Well. In that case. I've got tons of blankets and food and water and a radio and flares—"

"Will we need those?"

"Flares and radios? Nope. Blankets?" I raise an eyebrow.

"Did you order up this snowstorm?" she teases.

"If I'd known I could order up a snowstorm, I *might have*."

She leans a little closer, a small secret smile teasing over her lips. "Where are these famous blankets?"

I grin. "In the backseat."

"Are you saying I'd have to climb back there if I wanted one?"

"I'm saying if you climb into the backseat, I'd definitely make sure you were warm enough."

Even in the dim light of the snow-blanketed truck, I can see mischief play over her smile. I watch her perfect heart-shaped backside recede as she does exactly what I suggested.

I follow her back—not nearly as gracefully, almost landing in her lap, which makes both of us hoot with laughter. And just like that, it feels like we're back to where we were the first day we met, racing hand in hand to catch the last ten minutes of an act we were both dying to see because we'd misread the schedule, laughing for almost no reason because everything seemed brighter and funnier. The laughter dries up in my mouth, and I reach out a hand to push a few strands of hair back from her face. It's as smooth and silky as I remember.

And then she's not laughing, either, as she leans in and I do the same and our mouths meet. It's a messy, headlong clash, longing and delayed gratification making us both groan into each other. My hands weave into her hair, loving the smooth silk of the dark strands, while the other finds her waist through her parka. I want more, so much more, but I don't want to rush or scare her.

I'd forgotten Mika's not easily scared, though. She's needy, too, her hands on both sides of my face, pulling me in, her tongue hungry and avid. "God, Connor," she groans, pulling back just long enough to speak. "Is it crazy I feel like I *missed* this?"

No, no, it's not, I think. I don't say it, because I'm diving back into the kiss, clutching her close, drawing her over me, into my lap. She straddles me eagerly, finding me already so hard for her that it hurts. She feels so good, the weight of her against my straining cock, the heat between her legs enough that I can feel it through all the layers of cloth. My hand finds the bottom of her shirt and slides under. Her skin is soft as silk, every bit as smooth as it looks. As soon as the heat of my hand finds her ribs, she pants against my lips.

She breaks the kiss to wrestle her parka off, and I do the same with mine. Both land on the floor of the truck.

"Okay?" I ask, raising her shirt, and she nods.

"Yes, please," she says, and it makes me smile.

"Good, because I want to see you."

I pull her shirt over her head and I'm glad I did, because she's better than memory, better than fantasy. She's wearing a red lace bra with a tiny ribbon set right between her breasts.

I groan at the sight and dip my head to touch my mouth to the bare, sweet curve of her. Her nipple is hard under the lace, and my fingers can't stay away, sweeping back and forth over the needy, sensitive tip, teasing it to even more of a peak. She's whimpering now, and rubbing herself against me.

"Chasing that missing orgasm?" My own voice is rough. I'm a lot more wound up than I thought I could get after a few minutes of kissing. Mika did this to me last time, too—part of why things ended... unequitably. But I'm older and wiser, and I can't think of anything I want more than to watch her come undone. "Let me see the panties," I command.

Her hands fumble with the button of her jeans. I take over, unfastening her and groaning when I see that, yes, thank God and Santa and the Grinch and Christmas Yoda, she's wearing matching red lace panties. I slide a hand into them, finding her wet and swollen. I ease a finger up to where she needs me most, circling her clit. She bangs her head back against the soft leather of the seat, and her tongue comes out, wetting her lips. I have to kiss her again, and I kiss her and kiss her until she trembles and falls apart under my circling finger, groaning her release into my mouth. When she finally breaks the kiss, shaking and sighing, she presses her cheek against mine and wraps her arms around me in a hug that feels almost as good as making her come.

I stroke her back for a few minutes, which means I feel the exact moment when regret comes for her. She stiffens.

"You okay?"

She pulls back and lifts her head. "I just—I promised myself I wouldn't do this."

"Do what?"

"I have this tendency to be impulsive. Make… mistakes."

"Are you calling me a mistake?" I tease.

She won't quite meet my eye, so I tip her chin up to look at her. She bites her lip. "We live on opposite coasts and we're not in any position to see each other again," she says.

I can't argue with her, even though a small, stubborn part of me really wants to. Instead I say, "That part's true. But I'm still glad this happened. I hope it was worth waiting for—that was a long wait to get yours."

Now she's smiling. "It was *definitely* worth it. You were right. About paying your debts with interest."

We grin foolishly at each other.

She leans her head against my shoulder again. Her body relaxes back to its limp-with-pleasure state, trusting in my arms.

It's pretty fucking awesome.

After another minute, she lifts her head. "I've had more fun today than I have… maybe ever, honestly? And I feel more like myself today than I have in a long time. So… thank you."

My chest inflates like Christmas Yoda, and my heart feels like it has After-Grinch proportions. "No," I say, my voice even rougher than earlier. "Thank you. I was basically dreading Christmas this year. All the family togetherness, all the couples, and *me*. And you've redeemed it for me. You've made it feel like Christmas."

She snuggles closer.

Outside the truck, the sky lightens and the snow lessens, but the feel of her arms around me is better than better-than-sex cake, and I'm in no hurry to move.

CHAPTER 9
MIKA

Cuddling with Connor, wrapped in a blanket in the backseat of his truck was not on the list of things I thought I'd do today. Gift wrapping? Yes. Baking (badly)? Possibly. Basking in a post-orgasm glow with a sexy man on the side of the road in a snowstorm? Not in a million years. And yet...

It feels great, and that's not just the post-coital endorphins talking. Connor feels...right. My initial awkwardness aside, everything between us has been easy. Including the way he's gently poking fun at me as I explain the rationale for my matching underwear.

"My mom always said you put yourself together from the inside out. If you're wearing a tatty bra and granny panties, you don't carry yourself as confidently." I shrug, because I never questioned my mom's mantra, even when I was the only girl in gym class with a La Perla training bra. My mom didn't consider it a luxury, and my dad didn't want to know, so I grew up believing good lingerie is a necessity.

"So you still believe that, obviously?" Connor runs a

finger over the silky strap of my bra, and I will his hand to drift lower.

"Obviously." I grin up at him. "Do you have a complaint about my under things, Mr. Perez?"

"Absolutely not." Connor laughs and leans over to kiss me.

He's just swept his tongue over my bottom lip, and I'm shifting to maybe possibly climb on his lap again, when there's a banging on the window that causes both of us to jerk back. I grab for the blanket. Good thing, because in the next minute, the door swings open and Rachel and Brody are standing there, brows furrowed and arms crossed.

"What the hell are you doing here?" Connor shifts away from me, straightening the collar of his flannel shirt.

"What the hell are *you* doing?" Rachel's tone is halfway between accusatory and puzzled.

"Dude, what's this?" Brody asks.

I don't know Brody well at all. Rachel insists he's amazing and he's been super nice to me. But right now, he's intimidating as hell, whether he means to be or not. I shrink back into my blanket.

Rachel frowns. "I tried to call but you weren't answering. We were worried about you so I tracked your phone. I thought you got stuck in the snow," she tells Connor. Maybe she hasn't noticed me yet. "I saw you weren't moving and I thought you'd gone off the road. Obviously not."

Her gaze darts over Connor's shoulder. So much for not noticing me.

"We left the Merrithrifts and a squall came through, so we pulled over to be safe," Connor says.

"Looks like that's not all you pulled over for," says

Brody. The corner of his mouth twitches up. Does he think this is funny? That's unexpected, but better than the alternative.

"Guys, close the damn door. It's freezing." Connor reaches for the handle. He pulls the blanket with him, exposing my red bra and eliminating any doubt about what we were doing. I scramble for the blanket again, but it's pointless.

Rachel's eyes take in my state, then rise up to my face. "Mika..." She gives me a sympathetic look.

She doesn't have to say it. I hear the words she doesn't utter. *That pact you made to yourself, to stop getting involved with guys who weren't ready to be serious, didn't last long, did it?*

"Seriously, Connor?" Rachel's tone is hard as she turns her attention to her brother. "After what you pulled on Brody and me? I know you think you're just having fun, but Mika's vulnerable right now. She doesn't need your flavor-of-the-week shenanigans."

Connor's flavor-of-the-week shenanigans? I don't know exactly what that means, but Rachel's right about breaking my promise to myself. Here I am again, getting naked with a guy who, if Rachel's words and tone are to be believed, isn't in the habit of being serious about anyone, let alone a woman who dropped in for the holidays from the East Coast.

Connor swings around to look at me and there's a helplessness in his expression. I feel like I should jump in and defend him—defend us—but I can't seem to make my mouth work. The humiliation of being caught with my pants literally down is too much.

He glances at me for another second before turning

back to Rachel and Brody and saying, "This isn't what it seems like. Mika and I—"

But then he clamps his mouth shut. And the look he gives me next is full of *I'm sorry.*

I've seen that look so many times before from so many guys.

My stomach clenches with hurt and disappointment. And that's the moment I realize: I've done it again. I've gone and hatched feelings for a guy who's just having a good time.

"I should probably go." Finally I find my voice. I reach for my sweater on the floor and pull it over my head. "Thanks for a great day."

"Mika, wait," Connor starts.

"No, really. I had a great day with you. I did." I grab my coat and fumble with the door handle. When I push the door open I jump out of Connor's truck, landing in snow that goes over my boots but I don't care. I'm embarrassed, and I need to get out of here.

"Mika," Connor calls.

Hearing my name from his lips again makes my stomach dip, but I continue around the truck until I'm standing behind Rachel and Brody. Rachel turns to glance at me. I don't know what she sees in my face, but she says, "I'm going to take Mika home. Brody, you go with Connor and make sure he gets out of here okay."

"I don't need a babysitter." Connor crosses his arms.

"You need a timeout and maybe a cold shower," says Brody, grinning. "Come on. Do you want me to drive?"

I hear Connor's voice, but I don't hear what he says as

Rachel puts an arm around me. "Come on. Let's get out of here."

I let her guide me to Brody's SUV. The wind whips my hair every which way and I'm glad because I know my conflicted feelings are all over my face, and I don't know which of them Rachel sees. Embarrassment about being caught fooling around with my best friend's brother. Remorse about making another impulsive decision.

Or regret that something so sweet has been ruined, and maybe I have no one to blame but my foolish heart.

I felt something for Connor. Scratch that, I feel something for Connor. But if I'm just another conquest to him, my feelings are not only ill-advised. They're irrelevant.

CHAPTER 10
CONNOR

"Deep breaths, Connor."

The doors have barely shut and the engine only just started when Brody issues his edict. But I've got a few other things on my mind.

"What the hell was that? An intervention? We're grown-ass adults."

I can feel the power of Brody's side-eye, even though I never take my own eyes off the road. "Doesn't feel so good, does it?" he inquires. "Getting called out about your love life?"

Something in his voice makes me cast a glance his way, and—yes, he's laughing. "Are you *laughing* at me?"

"Hell yes, I'm laughing. Do you *remember* pulling me aside and taking a layer of skin off over my being with Rachel? She's pissed because you're a hypocrite, dude."

"You're right," I tell Brody, because he totally is. "I had that coming, big time."

Brody huffs out a self-satisfied half-laugh. "Okay," he says. "Now we've got that out of the way. Tell me what the fuck was going on back there. Because I know you well enough to know you're too smart to get happy-naked with Rachel's bestie without having a pretty damn good reason."

I tell him the whole story. How I met Mika when I visited Rachel in college. How we went to the music festival together and it was one of those days that freezes forever in your memory.

We kept splitting off from the group only to meet up again at an act we both wanted to see. Or running into each other waiting in line at the same Ethiopian food stand. Each time, it felt less like coincidence and more like fate, and eventually, without even hashing it out, we stuck by each other's sides, until her hand brushed mine and I grasped it and didn't let it go. She was so cute, the way she mouthed the words to the songs, too shy to sing them out loud in case she got them wrong, and wiggled her hot little ass because she wasn't the dance-like-no-one's watching type. But then later, when no one was watching, she didn't hold back in my arms, and it felt like the best gift ever, wrapped in gold paper and tied with a hundred perfect ribbons.

I think of the look on Mika's face when Rachel said the thing about my flavor-of-the-week shenanigans. I wish I could claim that comment was totally out of line, but to be absolutely fair? Long term has never been my relationship MO.

But that's partly because no one ever made me feel like sticking around. And Mika? She does.

Or she did, before Rachel scared the hell out of her. Made her think I was another one of her mistakes. She didn't look back as Rachel hustled her into the SUV—not once.

I can still see the abandon on Mika's face when she tumbled into her release, can still feel the flutter of her sex against my fingers. Most of all, I can still hear her voice, shy and pleased, telling me she had the best day she'd had in a long time, that she'd felt more like herself than she had in ages.

It makes me wish we'd known, that day of the music festival years ago, what it meant to feel so alive. Maybe then we wouldn't have slunk back to our corners and let years pass before we connected again.

"I like her, Brody. I like her so fucking much."

I can feel him watching me.

"But she lives on the East Coast! And I'm not sure I know *how* to not be a mistake for someone."

"Been there," he says. Super quiet. Not making a point, not telling me how to feel. Just: You're not the only one.

"I don't exactly have a history of long-term relationships."

"Neither did I before Rachel," he reminds me. "I thought I knew who I was before Rachel. But Rachel made me want to be who *she* thought I was. The good guy she saw."

"I don't think Mika thinks I'm much of a good guy, after what just happened."

"Let me ask you something," Brody says. "Do you mean she doesn't think you are? Or you're afraid you can't be who she sees?"

That's the thing about Brody, the trait that makes us best friends—he listens and hears not just what I'm saying, but also what I'm not saying. I huff out a breath. "You might be onto something."

"Can I tell you what I know about this?"

"Yeah," I say.

"There's a lot I don't fucking know. I don't know how the future turns out or whether you guys end up together or what happens with the long distance. But I do know that when you're ready to not be a mistake? You're going to do a great fucking job at it. You have a huge heart and you take care of the people you love. You're fierce. She'd be lucky to have you decide not to be her mistake."

My heart that grew three sizes today almost can't take it, but I haven't cried in front of another guy since I was nine, and twenty-first century emotional maturity can go fuck itself; I'm not going to start now.

"Thanks, man," I say, but we both know what I mean. I'm sure of it.

We lapse into silence then, and I think about the day. The jokes about Nan's scary collection of gifts, the better-than-sex-cake, the awful wrapping jobs, Mika's hands over mine, her mouth under mine, every curve of her body and needy whimper.

And then I think about the Merrithrifts and how much they love doing Christmas, how even now, when they can't climb ladders, they find a way to do Christmas together and take so much joy in it.

Maybe when you find the person who's like that for you, you know.

Maybe I know. And maybe I know what I need to do.

"I want to not be her mistake," I tell Brody.

"I know," he says, and I can hear the smile in his voice.

CHAPTER 11

MIKA

Rachel turns on the radio as we drive. She doesn't chide me or even ask what was happening when she and Brody burst in on Connor and me in his truck. Some might say this is because she's an amazing friend. Which she is. But I'm pretty sure she's not saying anything because she feels sorry for me. She thinks Connor took advantage of me, and I'm too raw to correct her.

Did he take advantage of me? It didn't feel that way, and his surprise at Rachel's accusations was genuine. He was caught off guard and defensive, which isn't the hallmark of a guy who was just getting his rocks off. I feel like if Connor *were* doing that, he'd own it like he owns his terrible singing and even worse gift-wrapping skills.

Let's add to the fact that the orgasm inequality this time was firmly in my favor. I mean, I was the one writhing with pleasure. Not him. Although he definitely looked like he was enjoying himself. And enjoying me. It's been so long since I've felt the kind of connection with someone that I felt with Connor today. I daresay the last time I felt this way was with Connor in college. I can't be the only one feeling this way. Can I?

I don't realize Rachel has pulled up to an unfamiliar house until she puts the car in park and pockets the keys. Confused, I look over at her. "I need to pick up Justin," she reminds me. "We're at Gabe and Lucy's."

I remember Lucy's one of the women we met this morning at Rent-an-Elf. "Gabe's one of Brody's brothers?"

"Yeah, and Lucy's husband, in case that wasn't obvious."

"Got it." I settle in my seat, fully intending to stay in the car. The last thing I want is to see anyone—let alone a happy couple.

But Rachel says, "Are you coming?" and I make myself follow her. I can't find a reasonable excuse to stay in the car. Even if I could, Rachel wouldn't let me.

She knocks on the front door and pushes it open without waiting for a response. We enter into a black-and-white tiled foyer, and I hear Christmas music and kids giggling. Rachel slips off her snowy boots and hangs her coat on the rack. I do the same and we pad down the hallway to the kitchen.

Lucy and Mari are sitting at the kitchen table decorating cookies with Justin, Rachel's adorable toddler almost-step-son, and a girl I don't recognize. A baby is crawling on the floor, pulling at the ears of a large dog who looks resigned and a little tired.

"Hey, welcome, welcome," says Lucy. "You're just in time to help us finish the cookie decorating. It's pretty spectacular, right?"

"It's amazing," Rachel gushes. She goes to perch on the edge of the chair with Justin, who giggles when she uses sprinkles to add eyes and a mouth to his red and green Christmas tree cookie.

I smile and lean against the counter, happy to fade into the background until Mari says, "You look like someone kicked your dog. Are you okay?"

Her casual words make my eyes sting, and Lucy hurries to my side. "Oh, Mika, what's wrong? What happened?"

I don't want to spill my guts in front of the kids—little pitchers have big ears and all that—but suddenly I want to talk about what happened. I need to say it out loud. I tilt my head towards a door in the corner of the kitchen and Rachel, Mari, and Lucy follow me.

It turns out the door leads to the laundry room. There are worse places for true confessions than in the company of a front-loading Maytag and three sympathetic listeners. My words tumble out. "I hooked up with a guy." Rachel shoots me a look and I add, "Connor. I hooked up with Connor."

"Wow. And that's a bad thing?" asks Lucy.

"Yes. No." I bite my lip and shoot a glance at Rachel. "The thing is, it wasn't exactly the first time."

"What does that mean?" Rachel's brow furrows.

"Remember that music festival we went to our sophomore year of college?" I ask and Rachel nods. "Connor and I hooked up that night. It was no big deal at the time—we lived too far apart to even talk about seeing each other again. But seeing him here feels like we've gotten a second chance."

"Do you want a second chance with my brother?" Rachel doesn't look pissed, just confused.

"Maybe?" I bite my lip.

"For what it's worth, Connor is hot," offers Mari. Then she glances at Rachel and says, "Sorry. But he is."

"La, la, la, la, not listening," Rachel says. She turns to me. "Why *maybe*?"

"I was really enjoying being with him again. But then you and Brody showed up and you talked about Connor always hooking up and…" I scrunch up my nose like I smelled something bad. "I have this habit of choosing the wrong guys, and I honestly don't have the stamina for it anymore. I want a good guy for a change."

"Wait," Rachel says. "Brody and I talked about Connor always hooking up?"

"You said something about his flavor-of-the-week shenanigans."

"Ohhh," Rachel says. She claps her hand over her mouth. "That's not what I meant. Connor doesn't really have long-term relationships, but he's not a dog. He's definitely not one of those guys who's chronically on bed rotation."

"Connor is a good guy," says Lucy. "I need to put that out there since he's not here to speak for himself."

"But is he a good guy for *me* or is he another bad decision I'm going to end up paying for in tears and self-recrimination?" I give a wobbly smile. "That's my go-to. Has been for years now. And in fairness, he doesn't owe me anything. I live on the East Coast. I'm visiting for a few days. He would be entirely within his rights to assume I was just looking for a good time."

"Are you?" Lucy asks, at the same time Mari asks, "Do you feel like today was a mistake?"

I look at the women surrounding me. They're all leaning in, like they're ready to catch me if I fall, and the expression on each of their faces is full of concern, not judgment. I shake my head as the realization begins to dawn on me. "I don't think anything about today has been a mistake."

"Not even Connor?" Rachel asks.

I hesitate because I'm so used to keeping the fact I hooked up with Connor from her. But then I look at her, really look. This is my friend Rachel. She's *never* told me anything I did was a mistake, even when I was sure it was. She's supported me through everything—and she's brought me here to be with these women who are supporting me, too.

"Not even Connor," I say, feeling sure of myself for the first time in a long time. Maybe I've been too hard on myself in calling all of my past experiences mistakes. Maybe I've just been practicing for when it really mattered.

Rachel's face blooms into a big smile, and she reaches for my hand. "I say then what are you going to do about it? Because if I know my brother, he's freaking out."

"You're not mad?" I ask.

"I was never mad." She squints. "At you, anyway. Connor's another matter. I'm planning to give him hell about being a hypocrite for the rest of his life, because I'm his sister, and I can." Rachel's smile softens. "But no. If you're with Connor, at least I know I already love you. I wouldn't have to pretend for the sake of family harmony."

"Well, I'm not with Connor." I gesture vaguely to the

laundry room. "Obviously." And then I look around the circle again, at their amused, gentle expressions. "Why the hell am I not with Connor?" I demand.

There's an explosion of laughter from my new friends.

"I guess you need to go find him? There are at least three people in this room who know where he lives," says Lucy. "Just saying."

I glance at them, and for the first time since Rachel and Brody opened the door of Connor's truck I feel my lips tilt up and I say, "Okay. So who's driving me?"

RACHEL DRIVES me to Connor's house because that's where his phone says he is. When we let ourselves in, we note that it smells like him but is conspicuously empty except for Connor's dog, Nellie, snoring in front of an empty fireplace. Connor's phone, unfortunately, is on the coffee table.

"He's not here," says Rachel, tapping at the screen of her cell phone. "I'm texting Brody but he's not answering. Let me try to call him."

As she brings the phone to her ear, I take the opportunity to look around Connor's living room. It's very masculine—there's a brown leather couch and a giant TV in the corner—but there's also a bookcase full of books and photos scattered on the mantle. I can't decide which I'm drawn to more. Maybe the idea bel of learning what Connor loves to watch on his big TV and what books have changed his life. If I'm lucky enough to get the chance to find out.

"He's not answering," Rachel says, shoving her phone in the pocket of her coat. "I have no idea where they'd be."

Well, if Rachel doesn't know, I definitely wouldn't. My stomach thuds to my knees. Is that how this ends? Not with a bang but with an empty living room and voicemail?

"Let's go to Carol-oke," says Rachel. She's doing that thing where she's making her voice high and bright. My stomach sinks another couple of inches.

"What is Carol-oke?"

"It's the culmination of the Rent-an-Elf event and Brody and I had talked about going. It's karaoke, but all the songs are Christmas-themed. It's fun. There are candy cane shots, if all else fails." Rachel smiles. "If Brody and Connor are there, it's definitely too loud to hear a phone notification."

Christmas karaoke sounds like my worst nightmare, but I nod. If there's a chance Connor might be there, I'll go. Aloud I say, "It's worth seeing if they're there, right?"

Although when we walk into the Depot Hotel lobby fifteen minutes later, I'm not so sure. Carol-oke is loud. And crowded. Did I mention that it's loud? The elves from the Rent-an-Elf event are still in costume, dancing in a circle to someone's (pretty bad) rendition of Slade's *Merry Christmas Everybody* and kids are running around like they've had a year's worth of sugar in an hour.

Rachel takes my hand and leans in, saying, "Let's see if we can find your guy."

"Rachel." I look at her. "Connor is your brother."

"And if he makes you happy, I'm here for it." Rachel's expression is stern. She doesn't wait for me to respond. She pulls me through the crowd and I scan faces, looking for Connor.

We're over by the cake table—Nan's better-than-sex cake is nearly gone—when I see him. His shoulders are the first thing I notice. That red flannel is like a beacon. Then he turns and I see his face. His brown eyes meet mine and I hold my breath. There are four feet between us, tops, and I'm the one who needs to close the gap. But I take a step toward him and he turns away.

If I thought my stomach sank earlier when Connor wasn't at his house, that's nothing. I swear, it's resting in the soles of my feet now, along with my heart. I guess that answers my question, doesn't it?

Rachel's chatting with Nan, and I'm about to tap her on the shoulder to get me out of here when someone at the microphone clears their throat. Great, another Carol-oke attempt. If it's *Grandma Got Run Over By a Reindeer* I might scream. Or cry. I feel dangerously close to doing both.

"Um, if I could have your attention." The voice comes over the microphone and I jerk my head up. Holy shit. It's Connor. "This one's for you, Mika."

I can't swallow. I'm not sure I can even breathe. My stomach has floated from the soles of my feet to my throat and now I'm almost positive I'm going to cry. And that's only from Connor calling me out on stage. *Then* he starts singing Mariah Carey's "All I Want for Christmas is You," and I can't help it. The tears flow like spring rain.

Not because Connor is good. Honestly, he's terrible. His voice is off-key, he has the lyrics all wrong, and he's slightly behind the music with his words. But he's singing. To me. In front of all of Rush Creek.

Rachel comes over and squeezes my hand, and I squeeze back like my life depends on it. But, truthfully, I'm hardly aware of it. All I can focus on is the man on stage singing. No one in my life has ever done something like this for me before. It's not only the singing, it's the grand gesture of it all. And the fact that Connor looks at no one but me. The look on his face answers every question and tells me everything I need to know. About Connor, his feelings and what I mean to him.

If that's not a gift, I don't know what is.

CHAPTER 12
CONNOR

As soon as the song ends, I jump down from the stage. For the first time since I started singing, I'm not blinded by the stage lights and I can see Mika clearly. What I see turns my heart to stone in my chest and freezes me in my tracks. Mika's face is buried in Rachel's shoulder, and she's crying.

Oh, shit. She doesn't feel the same way. Why should she? She's red lace and tiny perfect ribbons, and I'm...

Wrinkled end-flaps and too much tape.

My first impulse is to race for the exits. But my feet won't obey.

Mika lifts her face. And what I see there changes everything. She's smiling through her tears. Smiling at me. Me, Connor Perez, with my off-key singing and my shitty wrapping job and my homegrown grand gesture. She's smiling at me like I flew her to Paris for the weekend. My stone heart melts, and I'm filled with so much happiness I'm surprised I don't glow like Rudolph's nose.

She takes a step toward me, and then another. I stand

there, still frozen, waiting for the moment when she throws herself into my arms. She veers past me and hoists herself up onto the stage.

As I watch, she grabs the microphone, calls a request to the Carol-oke DJ, and opens her mouth.

She's bad.

I mean, she's *really* bad. She's singing Taylor Swift's "Christmas Tree Farm," which is a song I happen to love, and she's way off key. Messing up the words even though she's reading them off the screen. In fact, if I didn't know there was a screen there, I would figure she was ad libbing the whole thing.

But I love the shit out of it. I love the little red barrette that holds back some of her hair and the red lace I know she's wearing under her clothes. I love the dark silk of her hair and the deep flush on her cheeks. I love the way she's wiggling her ass in a not-quite-dance.

I love that the girl who has it all together is letting herself screw up in front of a room full of people just to show me how she feels.

I climb back onto the stage and find my place—the best place in the world—by her side.

"You know how we almost fell out of the tree today? That's how hard I'm falling for you," I whisper to her.

She fumbles the next line of the song completely, so I pick up the lyrics and we sing the rest of the song together, my hands over hers on the microphone. And when we're done, she throws her arms around me and whispers, "I'm falling for you, too."

As soon as we climb down from the stage, we're swarmed by Wilders and Perezes and Wilder spouses and girlfriends and Wilder children who are old enough to be out this late at night, all of whom are urging us not, under any circumstances, to quit our day jobs, or begging us, please, please, please never to sing again.

"Happy for you, man," Brody says. Just that, but one of the things about Brody and his brothers is that even when there aren't a lot of words, there's a lot of love.

"Thanks," I say, and then we both give each other wry man-looks that say all the things we won't say out loud.

Rachel is hugging Mika, and Lucy and Mari are crowding around jumping up and down. And I look around at my whole family, my whole town, and merry fucking Christmas to me, because I can't believe I ever thought this sucked.

The next song starts up, and thankfully, it's one of the Wilder littles singing Rudolph, and everyone's too busy being proud parents and siblings and aunties and uncles to notice when Mika and I bundle ourselves into our coats and sneak out, into the softly falling snow. This time it's not a squall but a gentle flurry of fat flakes that settle in Mika's hair and on the collar of her jacket. She tilts her face up to catch the falling snow, and I couldn't stop myself if my survival depended on it: I drop my mouth to hers and kiss her until we're both breathless.

When someone's clearing throat reminds me that we're standing outside what's very much a family show, I release her—but not far. I wrap her hand in mine and squeeze, and I have no intention of letting go any time soon.

"Hey," I say.

"Hey yourself."

There are snowflakes in her hair. Her nose and cheeks

are red from the cold. She's never looked more beautiful to me. And I can't believe I ever walked away from her.

"I know you might already have family plans... but how would you feel about spending Christmas with me? And the Perezes. And the Wilders."

Her mouth falls open. "You're asking me to—to spend Christmas with your family?"

"Uh-huh. And stay the rest of your break, too, if you can."

"I would feel—like it was the best Christmas present ever."

I grin. "Yeah? Me? I'm your best Christmas present ever?"

"Yup," she says. "All wrapped up in silver paper and taped extra well, Connor-style." She gestures to indicate the amount of tape that goes into one of my wrapping jobs. Then she pauses, and one of those teasing smiles that I love so much tips up the corner of her mouth. "And I'm yours."

She leans in, rises up on her tiptoes, and presses her lips to my ear. "If you're super nice to me? I'll let you unwrap me."

"Is that a promise?" I grin down at her.

Mika's expression softens, and she nods. "Like I said, I'm all yours."

Same, Mika. Hard same.

As I lean down and kiss her again, I can't believe I was ever dreading this Christmas. Turns out, there's no place I'd rather be than Rush Creek, as long as Mika is by my side.

"They want the blue lights on that tree." I point to the pine tree in the Merrithrifts' front yard where my friends Lincoln and Evie are untangling a strand of lights. "Trust me, Rebecca and Wallace know what they want and where they want it."

"They'll make you redo it," Connor calls over with a laugh. "They're super nice, but Mika's right. These Christmas decorations mean a lot to them."

"Okay." Lincoln shrugs, and he and Evie sidestep over to the tree next to them, holding the strand of lights.

Connor and Brody are putting more lights on the roof —a new addition this year, according to Connor—and Rachel and I are in charge of the inflatables. It feels strange to have my best friends from Enita Springs and my best friends in Rush Creek all here, where everything began between me and Connor. But it also feels incredibly right.

I've been living in Rush Creek for six months now. Connor and I did the long-distance thing (can you say lots of phone sex?) but we agreed pretty quickly that we wanted to be together long-term. My moving to Rush Creek was the obvious choice, and not only because I was ready to take a giant step away from my law career. Since the move, I've opened an online shop selling my art. I still do some consulting for my old law firm, but it's freeing to be pursuing my passion for the first time in my life. Saying I love it is a massive understatement.

"Mika, come help me," calls Evie. "Lincoln is terrible at this."

"I am not." He tries to look affronted, but fails. "Okay, I am. We're going to get fired as elves at this rate."

"Elf HR is pretty forgiving," I tell him. "There's an Elf staffing shortage, so you'd pretty much have to wire yourself to the tree to get fired. But if you help Rachel wield the Grinch and Christmas Yoda, Evie and I will do lights." I laugh and head over to take the strand from Lincoln's outstretched arms.

"He's cute, but he's hopeless," says Evie with a grin. "Why did I marry him again?"

"You mean why are you going to marry him twice?" I raise my eyebrows because, yeah, my friends are one of those second-chance success stories. They got divorced, ended up working together, and fell in love again. Lincoln asked Evie to remarry him last Fourth of July and she said yes, but they're in no hurry to set a date.

"Speaking of the best decision I ever made." Evie lowers her voice. "You and Connor seem really happy. *You* seem really happy."

"I am. I love it here, and I love him. He's the yin to my yang, you know?" I can't help letting a contented sigh escape. "I think of all the guys I tried to make things work with before, and now I realize it was like trying to fit a square peg into a round hole."

"Ouch," Evie says with a wry laugh. "Well, Connor is great. Truly. And I can see why you love it here, although upstate New York has nothing on Rush Creek when it comes to snow." Evie passes me the strand of lights again to do my side of the tree. "Next thing you know, you're going to tell me you're learning to ski."

"I've taken a few lessons, but the verdict is still out." I make a face. I'm still trying to embrace winter outdoor activities in Rush Creek. Although I do like the warming up afterward part.

"Anyone up for a hot chocolate break?" calls Rebecca Merrithrift, crossing the snowy yard with a tray. Wallace shuffles behind her. He's got a cane this year, but his smile is just as bright.

Rachel and Lincoln rush over and take the tray from Rebecca as Brody and Connor climb down from the roof. Connor squeezes me against him, then accepts a steaming mug and says, "This is great. Thank you so much."

"Your Christmas decorations are beautiful," Evie tells the Merrithrifts. "Very festive."

"I think you mean over-the-top, don't you?" says Wallace with a smile. "We do love them, though."

"The roof this year is a nice touch," says Brody.

"The roof is a special addition this year," says Rebecca. "Shall we see how it turned out?"

It's gray and overcast and the daylight is fading, so it's as good a time as any to turn on the Christmas lights. Connor springs to life and says, "I'll go plug them in."

"Nope. I got it," Brody says, placing his empty mug down in the snow.

Connor puts an arm around me, rubbing a hand up and down my arm. Maybe he thinks I'm cold or maybe he had too much better-than-sex cake earlier because he's acting like a kid hopped up on sugar. Either way, no complaints from me about being closer to this guy.

Brody strides over to the side of the house and plugs in the lights. We all squint up at the roof. Rachel gasps first, followed quickly by me. Although my gasp is more like a yelp because spelled out on the Merrithrifts' roof in white Christmas lights is: *Will U Marry Me?* and Connor has dropped to one knee in the snow beside me.

I turn to him and sputter, "Oh my God. Did you? Is this? What?"

He grins and says, "I did. It is." Then his grin fades and his expression turns serious as he pulls a small blue box from his coat pocket. He opens it. Inside is the most gorgeous ring I've ever seen—a square yellow diamond surrounded by tiny white diamonds. Then he looks me in the eye and says, "Will you marry me, Mika? Will you make me the happiest man in Rush Creek and marry me?"

"Oh my God, oh my God, oh my God." I think I might hyperventilate, and my hands shake uncontrollably.

Connor takes the ring from the box and slips the glove from my left hand. His eyes are full of love and the steady, easygoing affection I've come to count on. "Will you? Marry me?"

"Oh my God, yes." My hand in Connor's grounds me, and I watch in awe as he slips the ring onto my finger. It fits perfectly, and I pull him up so I can kiss him, deeply and thoroughly.

I don't think about the fact that we have an audience until I hear our small crowd clapping. I break reluctantly away from Connor, staying wrapped in his arms, and turn to Rebecca, saying, "You knew about this?" My head swivels to everyone. "Did you all know about this?"

They nod, and there are grins all around. Rachel squeezes my arm and says, "Welcome to the family."

"Oh my God." I bury my face in Connor's jacket. "I keep saying that."

"I think you're allowed," says Connor. "I'm just relieved you said yes."

"As if there was any doubt I would." I laugh.

"You never know," says Lincoln. "Your friends have engaged in some pretty questionable marriage behavior." That makes me and Evie laugh again.

Then I turn to Wallace and Rebecca and say, "It's on your roof. Our proposal is on your roof."

"Connor asked us a few months ago if we'd mind. He thought it would be perfect since you rediscovered each other here last year," says Rebecca.

"Rediscovered is one word for it," mumbles Brody.

"It is perfect. But do you want us to take it down?" The Christmas lights season has just started. I'm not sure the Merrithrifts want our proposal lighting up their roof for weeks.

"Absolutely not," says Rebecca. "We're thrilled we can share this with you."

"And as I always say, there's no such thing as too much love at Christmas," adds Wallace.

Connor kisses my hair and I squeeze his waist. Wallace is right. There's no such thing as too much love at Christmas, and this Christmas is overflowing with love.

Thank you so much for reading *A Wilder Weekend*! If you want to read about Rachel and Brody (and find out how Connor got himself in trouble), grab *Walk on the Wilder Side*, the story of what happens when Rachel brings some surprise excitement onto Brody's Boat. Grab their good-girl, bad-boy, opposites-attract, best-friend's-sister story now!

Go to geni.us/WOTWS

Keep reading for an excerpt from *Walk on the Wilder Side*!

EXCERPT FROM WALK ON THE WILDER SIDE

RACHEL

On the day my life goes off the rails, the first sign of trouble appears at 9:18 a.m. That's when my boss hands me a chocolate-frosted donut and a cup of coffee.

I stare at her, confused, because Hettie has never brought me anything before, even though we share an office in the children's department of the library. She's a petite Black woman with corkscrew curls, a no-nonsense manner, and an iron hand. A good boss, but not a donut bringer.

She delivers the bad news quickly, like an experienced nurse giving a flu vaccine. I've been laid off, effective next month.

My position has been replaced city-wide by a kiosk equipped with artificial intelligence that can recommend books to patrons and read books out loud to children.

I stare at her with my mouth open. "Are you serious?"

She winces. "I'm afraid so."

"Does the kiosk wipe their noses if they cry? Does it remind them to wash their hands after they use the bathroom? Can it shelve every book in the YA section without having to look up the series order?"

"I'm so, so sorry, Rachel." Her face softens with pity and apology. "You've been amazing. The perfect employee, on every axis. You work hard, you're good with the patrons— big and little, I can always count on you, everyone likes you. This has nothing to do with you. It's all about money."

"I know," I tell her, because she looks as miserable as I feel.

"We'll miss you so much, Rachel," she says helplessly.

She tells me to take the rest of my notice period as paid vacation and sends me home.

I'm not one of those people who has a ton of stuff to pack up. I leave behind the office supplies, because the library never has enough money for good pens or staplers, and grab my coffee mug, my water bottle, my lip balm, my photos, and the small sign that hangs over my desk.

Stick to the Plan! it says. Then, below, in smaller letters: *(First, make a plan.)*

Oh, God, this *so* does not go with the plan!

I toss the donut in the trash can—no appetite—and drive home in a blur of panic. I've never not had a job. From the time I was a little kid, I was a good girl: respectful, obedient, high-achieving. I'm careful. I pay my bills early. I toe the line. I make plans. (And stick to them.) I had my first job lined up before I finished my library science program, which was part of my master plan:

1. 4.0 in high school
2. College
3. Grad school

4. Great apartment
5. The library job of my dreams
6. Awesome boyfriend
7. Meet the parents
8. Get engaged
9. Get married
10. Have two point five kids (I can't decide between two and three)
11. Live happily ever after

Getting laid off feels like getting a C on a test I studied really hard for. I can't even bring myself to call my parents or my best friend Louisa, because even though I know I didn't do anything wrong ("the perfect employee," Hettie said), I still feel oddly ashamed.

Okay, I tell myself, as I circle for parking near the Somerville apartment I share with my boyfriend, Werner (step six). I got laid off, and that sucks. Tonight, however, I will be able to check off number seven on the master plan. I am meeting my boyfriend, Werner's, parents. And meeting the parents is the perfect stepping stone to number eight.

Werner's and my one-year dating anniversary is just a few weeks from now, and I've been fantasizing that he'll propose.

Candlelit dinner, champagne, a ring box, or, better yet, a ring atop a chocolate lava cake or a tiramisu... And Werner on one knee, eyes glittering with love, telling me that since the moment he first saw me at the college alumni event and crossed the room to talk to me, he's known that this was where we were headed...

Then a nine-month engagement, a spring wedding, a

year of getting to know each other as man and wife, and the two-point-five kiddos (step ten)...

(I will make up my mind by then. I'm not planning to deal in fractional kiddos, I swear.)

The layoff is a minor setback, I tell myself. As a step in the plan, it isn't even essential to the success of the next few steps.

Whereas meeting the parents is key. And—silver lining—the early dismissal today gives me plenty of time to finish cleaning the apartment and make a few pies. It's only 10:22.

I slide my Prius into a skinny parking space and walk the three blocks to the two-family where Werner and I live. As I unlock the door and let myself in, I can smell the roast I left simmering in the slow cooker. And the cleaning products I used this morning as I started the process of making everything perfect for the parent visit.

I take another step and trip over something, a pile of black slinkiness on the foyer floor, a tossed-aside heap.

Absentmindedly, I bend down and pick it up.

It's a short, black skirt with a lacy hem. Pretty. Sexy.

My mind stops, like someone jammed a stick into the spokes of the hamster wheel.

This is not my skirt.

And then I hear the sounds. Two voices. One low, familiar, grunting, the other higher-pitched, whimpering.

My brain races to provide any possible explanation except the obvious one. And part of me must not want to know the truth, because I start making up reasons I shouldn't walk towards the grunts and whimpers.

There might be an intruder in our apartment.

Werner might be doing something private (all alone) (by himself) he doesn't want me to walk in on.

A dying animal somehow got into our bedroom?

Or it's just the television.

Despite my brain's attempt to save me from the truth, my feet carry me inexorably toward the bedroom door, past a woman's blouse and Werner's shirt, both discarded on the floor. By now, my denial is morphing into a slow-growing rage. I turn the knob. Push the door open.

I see Werner's pale butt first. I recognize it, somehow, even though I've never seen it from this angle. I know what it's doing, even though I've never seen it clenching and thrusting like that. We're not the type of couple that uses mirrors or makes videos of ourselves. We have plain vanilla missionary sex under the covers, because that's how we like it.

That's how Werner *said* he likes it.

Right now, however, he is standing at the side of the bed, pounding into someone who is on all fours on his—our—bed.

"What the *hell*?"

That's my voice. Which is remarkable for two reasons. One: I didn't mean to speak. And two: I never swear.

Werner yanks himself free of the woman underneath him so fast I'm surprised he doesn't break something, er, valuable. Which offers me a totally different unwanted backside view—ugh.

It takes the owner of this view a little longer than Werner to realize what's going on, but when she does, she gasps and grasps for anything she can find to cover herself. Even so, as she clutches Werner's quilt to her body, tugging it off the bed, I catch the front view: lacy red teddy and breasts pushed up to her chin.

Is that thing *crotchless*? my mind demands to know, despite the urgency and absurdity of the situation.

I've never seen her before, which is *very* slim relief.

"Get out," I snarl at her, and, to her credit, she gets, grabbing her clothes as she rushes out. I can hear her beginning to cry as she removes herself.

I'm alone with Werner now. He's desperately trying to get himself back into his tighty-whities. I guess it's a survival instinct, covering up your parts when you've been caught. He's red and breathless and saying my name, begging me.

"Rachel, please, it's not what it looks like."

"I don't think that's even *possible*." A weird calm settles over me. If someone turns out not to be the man you thought he was, can you fall instantly out of love with him?

If someone disappoints you completely, does he lose his power to break your heart?

Or am I just in shock?

Shock is the more likely option. But I plan to take advantage of the numbness and clarity of mind while it lasts. "You were having sex with another woman in *our* bedroom. It's exactly what it looks like."

The bedroom I never stopped thinking of as *his* bedroom, my mind observes.

Shut up, mind.

"Rachel, please, listen. You're the one who's meeting my parents tonight."

"Oh, my *God*, is that supposed to *help*? You've just shown me your butt. Literally! The butt of a man who'd have sex with one woman on the same day another one is cooking for his parents!"

"Rachel, please. *You're* the girl I want to marry."

Those words stop me cold for half a second. Because they are—were—the prize I coveted.

And then I come to my senses: Werner is not a prize.

He's a total and complete loser who just did the lowest thing a boyfriend can do.

"Sure." I barely recognize my voice. It is hard, dark, cynical. "She's just the girl you..."

But apparently I have used up my ration of curses this morning, and I don't finish the sentence.

"Rachel, listen to me. If you leave because of this, I'll never forgive myself. You're my perfect woman."

My perfect woman.

And what did Hettie call me at work today, just before I was replaced by a kiosk? *The perfect employee.*

Perfect.

Perfect.

What horse pucky.

This being perfect thing?

It's not working out for me.

Need more? *Walk on the Wilder Side* is available now!

Go to geni.us/WOTWS (QR code on next page)

ALSO BY SERENA BELL

Wilder Adventures

Make Me Wilder

Walk on the Wilder Side

Wilder With You

A Little Wilder

Wilder at Last

Hott Springs Eternal

Hott Shot

Hott Take

Some Like It Hott

Running Hott

Hott Hotter Hottest

Under One Roof

Do Over

Head Over Heels

Sleepover

Returning Home

Hold On Tight

Can't Hold Back

To Have and to Hold

Holding Out

Tierney Bay

So Close

So True

New York Glitz

Still So Hot!

Hot & Bothered

Standalone

Turn Up the Heat

Holiday Novella

After Midnight

ABOUT THE AUTHOR

USA Today bestselling author Serena Bell writes contemporary romance with heat, heart, and humor. A former journalist, Serena has always believed that everyone has an amazing story to tell if you listen carefully, and you can often find her scribbling in her tiny garret office, mainlining chocolate and bringing to life the tales in her head.

Serena's books have earned many honors, including a RITA finalist spot, an RT Reviewers' Choice Award, Apple Books Best Book of the Month, and Amazon Best Book of the Year for Romance.

When not writing, Serena loves to spend time with her college-sweetheart husband and two hilarious kiddos—all of whom are incredibly tolerant not just of Serena's imaginary friends but also of how often she changes her hobbies and how passionately she embraces the new ones. These days, it's stand-up paddle boarding, board-gaming, meditation, and long walks with good friends.

www.ingramcontent.com/pod-product-compliance
Lightning Source LLC
Chambersburg PA
CBHW060713190726
48289CB00002B/667